RUNAWAY
STALLION

RUNAWAY STALLION

by

Walt Morey

Blue Heron Publishing, Inc.
Hillsboro, Oregon

To Randy Litman and Little John —
and all the boys and girls who have asked,
"When are you going to write a horse story?"

- 1 -

THE TRAIN waited on a siding for the flyer to pass. A ramp was lowered from the special car and down came a bantam-sized man leading a sleek red stallion in a gold blanket. The words FLY-BY were appliqued in blue silk on the blanket.

The horse paced sedately the length of the train, Jerry, his groom, talking softly and quietly to keep him calm.

Surprised comments followed them: "Queer place to exercise a race horse." Had to, been cooped up too long." "Never thought I'd see him." "Made his owner rich." "Fastest horse in the country."

Three coaches from the engine, Jerry turned back. He didn't want the high-strung thoroughbred any nearer the fire-breathing monster. That moment the engine exploded in a thunderous blast of steam. The horse reared in terror. The halter rope was torn from Jerry's hands. Voices shouted, grooms and trainer ran. The horse lunged up the bank, raced across the level, and vanished into the dark forest.

Fly-by, the famous race horse, was lost in the primitive wilderness of the High Cascades.

Fly-by heard the shouting of familiar voices but he was intent on fleeing from the long white horror that licked out at him like the tongue of an angry snake. He plunged wildly through brush, around trees and rocks. In less than a minute the voices which might have calmed him were lost.

The dragging halter rope caught in the crack of a rock and jerked him up short. It delayed him only a moment. He reared

1

back, yanking and pulling with all his strength. The halter slipped off over his head.

He raced on.

The flapping gold blanket hindered Fly-by, but not for long. He shed it as he tore through a heavy patch of brush. Now he was running free. He shot out of the trees into a small cuplike valley, crossed it at breakneck speed, and entered the trees again. The land was flat and less brushy. Running was his life and he was in top racing form, a perfectly conditioned machine of bone and muscle.

He raced on.

The timber finally thinned out and disappeared. The stallion emerged on a high, barren ridge. He stopped to catch his breath and look about. He was so far away he didn't hear a whisper on the wind when the flyer passed, the passenger train still waiting on the siding.

It was the first time in his life that Fly-by had been in any space larger than a four-acre pasture. This new-found freedom was almost more than he could bear. When he got his wind he charged down off the ridge. He bowed his neck and tossed his head. He pranced and kicked up his heels, enjoying himself in being able to run and run, never having to stop or turn because of a white fence. He alternately walked and galloped until the light began to fade from the day. He began climbing steadily and finally came into a small valley in the hills. It was protected on all sides by snow-covered mountains. The air funneling down off the snow fields was sharp and laced with the heady scent of pine. The valley floor was belly deep in lush grass. A small pole shed squatted at the far edge of the trees. Fly-by galloped across the spongy earth to inspect it.

The shed was old. The walls leaned and bulged as if about to fall down. There were no delicious smells of fresh timothy hay or grain, or people. It was not white and antiseptically clean with a foot of clean straw on the floor. The place smelled musty and old. The thin coating of straw on the floor was black with age. The stallion looked about, then pawed at the thin coating of straw which was always his way of attracting attention. This

2

time no one came.

He returned outside and stood looking expectantly about. It was time for his last feed of the day. Any minute Jerry should appear with the sterilized pail filled with a mixed grain enriched with molasses and minerals.

Jerry would sing out, "All right, big fellow, here you are," and stand and talk to him while he ate.

Fly-by nickered and snorted impatiently when Jerry was a couple of minutes late. This time no Jerry came. Finally he walked away from the shed and began to nibble tentatively at the grass. He was getting very hungry.

The horse wandered about the little valley daintily taking a bite here, another there, getting his first experimental taste of the different plants he found. Those that were bitter or tough he soon learned to leave. He stopped at a small, crystal stream and drank his fill.

He was discovering sights and smells and occasional sounds such as he'd never known. A pheasant exploded out of the grass at his feet and he reared and jumped in surprise. A rabbit hopped off a few feet away, sat up, and studied Fly-by vigorously chewing a grass stem. Two deer trotted from the timber, stopped and looked at him, batlike ears snapping back and forth. Satisfied they went to eating and paid no further attention to him. Birds flitted through the nearby brush. A small doglike animal came stealthily into the valley, looked at the stallion, then at the deer, licked its chops, and disappeared.

Fly-by nibbled at swelling pussy willow buds and found them tasteless. In a low place along the stream he found yellow blooms and a big-leafed, inviting looking plant. But it was bitter to his mouth. Deep in the stiff stalks of last year's grass he found this year's tender shoots sweet and to his liking. He began hunting through the dead clumps for this new growth. Then the sky darkened and a fine, cold mist began to fall. The deer disappeared.

The stallion returned to the shed and lay down in the musty straw. Again he waited for Jerry to come rub him down and to bring fresh hay. Rain fell softly on the ancient shakes.

Water dripped steadily from the edge of the roof. Inside, the great horse who'd been pampered and cared for from the day of his birth lay completely dry, still somewhat hungry and utterly lost.

Under similar conditions, many horses raised and cared for as Fly-by would die of starvation or injury, or fall prey to some big animal. But the blood of more than three hundred years of breeding for strength, courage, speed, stamina, and intelligence flowed in his veins. Not even a deer could sustain his trained speed. And no animal in these mountains could surpass his intelligence or match the smashing power of his hooves.

He possessed one other quality which all animals have in varying degrees. It flowed particularly strong in the blood of Fly-by — the instinct to live. It is instinct that makes the bird build its nest in areas resembling its own plumage. Instinct makes the cougar lie in wait on a rock or limb over a trail to pounce on the back of the deer he cannot catch running on the ground. Instinct makes most deer avoid such dangerous overhangs. Instinct sends the goat to his high mountain lookout, the eagle to his lonely perch on a dead snag where he can search the surrounding country for food. As naturally, as unconsciously as breathing, these qualities came to the fore in Fly-by now entering the greatest struggle of his life — that of survival.

The fine rain had ended by morning. The day dawned gray and soggy. Again the horse stood in the shed entrance and looked across the rain-wet valley. He nickered for Jerry to bring him his morning feed, to talk to him, to carefully brush and curry his shining coat. When Jerry did not come he finally ventured into the fresh, wet grass and began feeding on the tender grass shoots. Three deer, two does and a buck with a great rack of antlers, came from the near brush and began to graze. Fly-by moved toward them for companionship. The four fed about the valley close together. A pale sun finally sailed above the surrounding peaks and the grass dried. The deer finished eating and lay down to rest and chew their cuds. Fly-by lowered himself a few feet away and rested, too.

The horse stayed in the small valley. The feed was good,

there was clear water to drink, and a dry shed to sleep in. Every day the three deer joined him and they fed together companionably.

The first few days he waited morning and night for Jerry. He pawed the dead straw impatiently, nickered and snorted. There came a morning when he did not wait but ventured forth and began to feed. From then on he no longer looked for the little man.

Here Fly-by made his first big adjustment to life in the wild. Instinctively he copied the deer, feeding and resting when they did. They showed him where the best grasses grew in the low spots touched by the sun. Following them he found the salt lick where the black earth supplied the same needed minerals that the salt block in his manager had. He soon learned to feed in the lee of a brush patch or a hill when the wind blew. A pheasant or rabbit exploding from under his nose no longer startled him. He chased the doglike animal that sometimes watched from the edge of the trees until it no longer appeared.

He learned to be constantly on the alert while feeding. Because of this he discovered the cougar.

The big cat had slunk into the valley and was creeping through the long grass toward the deer. Fly-by spotted him and instinctively recognized the menace. The stallion moved toward the cat unafraid.

The cougar crouched, tail lashing, spitting angrily. His favorite method of attack, to leap from some high spot onto the back of his prey, was foiled. And the horse was hundreds of pounds heavier. Here on the ground the cat was at a disadvantage. But he was tempted. The horse represented days of food.

The horse reared and snorted, ears laid back, teeth bared. The buck deer noted the disturbance and trotted forward to investigate. He lowered his head and shook his antlers menacingly. In the face of so much opposition the cat whirled and vanished into the trees.

There were days when rain fell cold as ice and wind came off the high snow fields with a biting edge. Fly-by fed only briefly then returned to the shed. The deer did likewise and vanished into the forest. The cared-for sleekness of the stallion's coat faded. Long hair came in as protection against the cold of this high country. Burrs became entangled in his tail and mane. But because he'd been in top racing condition the horse lost little weight.

One morning Fly-by awoke to a white world with flakes falling so thickly he could not see the opposite side of the little valley. What would prove to be the last storm of the season was upon him. The snow fell softly, beating the dead grass flat, making the tender shoots almost impossible to find. It was his first experience with snow. He thrust his muzzle into it, felt its coldness, and blew mightily. He tried eating it and found nothing but cold wetness in his mouth.

The deer appeared and spent some time pawing down through the snow. Finally they left, drifting out one end of the valley.

Fly-by followed.

They went down a barren ridge that gradually took them to the lower plains. The snow turned to rain. The air became warmer. Here they met other deer browsing on brush. The buck and two does joined them. Fly-by hunted up a glade where there was grass and fed hungrily. He rested in the dry needles under a huge fir tree.

Next morning the deer were gone. Fly-by traveled on, going gradually lower, feeding as he went. Days later he emerged onto the floor of an immense valley so wide the opposite side was lost in hazy distance. Here, in the dark of evening, he came upon his first farm. Buildings and fences were familiar. He followed the fence to a gate and found a half dozen horses. Three were young mares. Fly-by whinnied excitedly. One raised her head, then trotted to the gate. The other mares followed.

The four stood, heads close together, nickering and nipping at each other. As their soft noses touched a feeling such as he'd never known flooded over Fly-by. It was the age-old desire of every stallion to have his own band of mares. Only this flimsy gate stood in his way. Excitedly he pushed with his chest against it. He reared and struck with his front feet at it. Suddenly he whirled and lashed out with both hind legs. Boards cracked and splintered. He kicked again and again. Boards flew apart. The gate collapsed. The next moment he was inside.

A big black gelding trotted forward to investigate. Fly-by whirled prepared to fight. The gelding turned away. It took but a minute to round up the mares and drive them out over the broken gate. They were pounding across an open field when a man ran from the house. He yelled angrily, then stood there and watched the little band disappear.

The following night Fly-by stole a young mare from another pasture five miles away. A few nights later he raided another farm and stole two more. His small band was growing.

Fly-by stayed about the area. He had a band to care for now. The feed on the valley floor was good and there were other ranches with young mares to add to his band.

But trouble was brewing for him. Twice he tried to break into pastures and once into a corral full of horses within a hundred feet of a house. Each time he was heard and driven off. Once a gun was fired and he felt the sting of shotgun pellets. He learned another valuable lesson. Man had the ability to injure without getting close.

Word passed among the ranchers that a wild stallion had come down out of the hills and was smashing fences and stealing mares. He was said to be big and powerful and could run like the wind. A search to capture was organized.

It took several days to locate Fly-by and his band. Then a trap was built at the end of a narrow ravine, and a crew of picked riders moved in.

They were feeding far out on a plain. Fly-by stood guard on a small rise. He saw the line of riders appear in the distance and move slowly forward. For a time he paid them scant attention. But they continued to move nearer. Finally he came down from the mound, rounded up his band, and drifted them toward the distant mouth of a ravine. The next he knew the riders were coming on fast. He took immediate alarm and ran at the mares, nipping and hazing them toward the ravine.

Riders burst from the cover of trees on either side and

charged them shouting, waving hats, coats, and lariats. Several fired guns. Fly-by surged to the lead and led his little band at an all-out gallop into the ravine and straight into the waiting trap. Two men rushed up, slid poles across the opening, and the band was imprisioned.

The mares were calm but Fly-by was frightened and angry at all the racket. He charged around the pole fence, running into it with his chest, rearing to strike at it with his front feet, looking for a way out. Riders raced up and dismounted.

Then, as he'd done with the gates, Fly-by whirled and let fly at the poles with his hind feet. Wood jumped and cracked at the impact. A top pole bounced out of its socket. The second broke at the small end and fell. The stallion spun about and sailed over the remaining poles. Men shouted and ran. A rope snaked out, struck the side of his head, and fell.

Riders charged in from either side to cut him off. But Fly-by turned on the marvelous speed that had carried him to eighteen wins in twenty-one big races. He left the riders far behind. A single horseman shot out of the near brush and tried to head him off. With a squeal of rage he charged them, ears laid back, teeth bared. The terrified horse bolted in the opposite direction and he was past. He thundered up the ravine, entered the brush, and began climbing in lunging bounds. He didn't stop until he emerged on a rocky point high above. None of his band had followed. A man had jumped into the breach he'd kicked in the trap, and because they were tame farm animals and mares they hadn't run him down.

A single shot sounded far below and something passed close with an angry buzzing sound. Fly-by turned and disappeared over the ridge. He did not look back.

In the following days Fly-by was guided only by his own desires and curiosity. He poked into shallow draws and mile-deep canyons. He dallied in glades and raced through mile after mile of virgin forests. He climbed hills and jumped rocks and logs and narrow, deep ravines that would have terrified Jerry and his trainer for fear he'd fall and break a leg. But the stallion came through with nothing more than an occasional scratch or a leg that was lame for a couple of days. His wanderings took him into lush valleys, then again into the high country where he waded in snow. He came upon no more ranches, and not once did he see another horse.

Finally he dropped down a long series of ridges to the floor of another broad valley that was bisected by a large, swift-flowing river. Here he again found fences and ranches. It was here that he experienced his first thunderstorm.

The clouds had been rolling and tumbling all afternoon. By evening they blanketed the sky. Bright flashes lit the night. Thunder grumbled in the distance. Rain began, driven by a gusty wind.

Fly-by came through the brush, crossed a broad, open field, and approached a white house with a lane which led down to a small neat, white barn. A white board fence enclosed a corral and pasture. It looked inviting. His own stable had been white like this. The fence enclosing his four-acre pasture where he'd run and kicked up his small heels from the time he was a colt had looked like this. For the first time in many weeks he thought of Jerry, his own warm box-stall layered with deep, clean straw, the bucket of grain, the fresh hay packed into the corner manger. Mostly he remembered Jerry's hands rubbing him down and the little man's soft, crooning voice talking to him. He was standing there looking when the storm let loose with fresh fury. Wind struck him a savage gust, driving rain pelted him like fine shot. Jagged lightning lit the dark sky and thunder crashed over the mountains.

Fly-by galloped past the house, down the lane, and slid to a halt at the gate. He nickered loudly for someone to come let him in out of the storm. He pawed impatiently at the gate and nickered again. A bright bolt of lightning tore the sky open. The drenched earth was bright as day. Thunder crashed over his head. He whirled in terror and bolted up the lane, fleeing blindly from this monster that shook the earth.

- 2 -

THE STORM woke Jeff Hunter. He lay snug and warm in bed under the eaves of the second floor and listened to the savage orchestration. Lightning flashed, thunder rolled and crashed. Rain drummed on the roof. Storms in the country were scarier than in the city.

A particularly bright flash bathed the room. Thunder exploded over the housetop fairly shaking the building. Jeff jumped out of bed and ran to the streaming window. He could see the black lacework of the maple limbs whipping in the wind, the vague outline of the barn beyond. A jagged slash ripped the night. He glimpsed a drenched world, the barn and fences, the pasture — and something else. A horse stood at the end of the lane, head over the gate as if it wanted to get into the barn out of the storm. Then the light was gone.

He waited for the next flash. Something had spooked the horse. He was racing up the lane. He was almost under the window. Jeff had a glimpse of a powerful glistening body, rippling muscles and long, driving legs. The head was up. Mane and tail streamed in the wind. Then darkness snatched the picture away.

Jeff gripped the windowsill. Excitement raced through him. The next flash showed only a soggy world and the empty lane. He crouched there watching the storm, until the night's chill drove him back to bed. For a long time sleep would not come. That glimpse of the racing horse was burned into his mind.

His first waking thought was of the horse, and he ran to the window. The storm had passed. The late winter sun was bright on a soaked world. Pools of water were diamond bright in the velvet green of the pasture. Jewel-like drops hung from the tips of the fresh-washed maple limbs.

There was no horse. He hadn't expected one.

Trixie came from the barn and stood looking at the new day placidly chewing her cud. His father was striding up the lane carrying a full pail of milk.

Jeff kept staring out the window lost in last night's vision.

His mother's voice jolted him, "Jeff! Time to get up."

"All right," he shouted. He threw on his clothes and pounded down the stairs into the warm kitchen. The room was filled with the mouth-watering aromas of frying bacon, eggs, toast, and hot cereal. His father sat at the table. His mother was dishing up the bacon and eggs at the big wood stove.

Lilian Hunter was of average height. Her slim body and smooth cheeks, flushed by the heat of the stove, made her seem younger than her thirty-five years. Her blue eyes were big and direct. She had always been a calm, cheerful person. But the last year, since they'd moved from the city to the valley, Jeff had noticed she seemed disturbed. He caught her frowning often and her voice was sometimes sharp. Her blonde hair, meticulously combed and piled on her head even at this early hour, made her seem taller than she was.

Jeff headed for the kitchen door but his mother's voice stopped him, "Where are you going?"

"Just outside."

"Breakfast's ready."

"I'll only be a minute."

"It can wait. Wash up and come eat."

Jeff hesitated and his father asked. "What's so important out there?"

Jeff pretended not to hear. He noisily washed at the sink and slicked down his straight brown hair. He felt his father's eyes studying him as he slipped into his chair. He carefully looked away.

Fred Hunter was almost the exact opposite of his wife. He was tall, with a heavy-boned, rugged frame. His hair was jet black. His black eyes could be sharp and stormy. He was a friendly man, but there was a stubborn set to his blunt chin. He would meet trouble head on.

Lilian put a steaming bowl of cereal on his plate and Jeff grumbled, "Oatmeal again?"

"You can have bacon and eggs afterward." She was a firm believer that a thirteen-year-old boy who was what his father called a "string bean" needed a hot cereal to put meat on long, growing bones.

Jeff sugared the cereal, drowned it in milk, and began shoveling it in. Lilian said surprised, "Stop eating so fast! What's got into you this morning? You're wound up like a spring."

Jeff caught his father's black eyes on him and mumbled, "There was a horse here last night."

"Well, there's horses all over the valley," Fred pointed out. "It's not so strange that one might get loose and show up here."

"This horse isn't from the valley."

"Oh? You've seen every horse in the valley, I take it."

"No, but I've seen a lot around Alderman's Blacksmith Shop and our store. They all look about the same."

"That's true enough except for Lem Decker's," Fred agreed. "Everybody says he's got the best horseflesh in the valley."

"He should have," Lilian said. "He's the wealthiest rancher around. The only one that has a hired man."

"Anyway," Fred said, "a loose cayuse showing up here is nothing to get steamed up about."

Jeff said nothing. Lilian watched him a minute then asked, "What was the horse like, Jeff?"

Jeff stopped eating. He began to smile and his gray eyes turned dreamy as he visualized again the big horse plunging up the lane through the storm.

12

Fred listened to his description and shook his head, "You're right, there's no such horse in this valley." He glanced at Lilian. "From the day we got here he's been yelling for a horse. Now he's even dreaming about one."

"I didn't dream it."

"In the middle of the night and during a storm you saw all those details about a horse?" Fred pointed out. "And such a horse!"

"The storm woke me," Jeff explained. "I was looking out the window and saw him in the lightning flash."

"I was awake, too," Lilian said. "Some of those flashes were as light as day."

"I saw no tracks in the lane when I went to milk."

"Were you looking for them?"

"All right. So maybe there was a cayuse here."

"It wasn't a cayuse," Jeff insisted.

"And it wasn't the grand animal you described."

Jeff shook his head. He couldn't admit he wanted to find the tracks so he could prove to himself such a marvelous horse did exist. "I just wanted to look," he said.

"To convince yourself he'd really been here?" Lilian smiled.

"I guess so." Jeff couldn't look at his father. He knew he was annoyed. He had been begging for a horse for months.

Fred Hunter didn't leave to open the store as usual right after breakfast. He sat and nursed his cup of coffee until Jeff finished his egg and toast. Then he said, "Suppose we look at those tracks."

The tracks were there, close together where the horse had gone down the lane, farther apart and deep where he'd come galloping back. Jeff put his hand in the soft mud of the spring and again he visualized the horse thundering up the lane as if he were a part of the thunder and lightning itself. Excitement began to build in him.

"There was a horse here all right," Fred said. "And from the distance between these tracks he was really traveling coming up the lane."

"He was big. He was — " Jeff searched for a word to describe him. "He was beautiful," he murmured. "He could run like — like the wind."

"Whoever lost him is probably out looking for him now." Fred rose, "Come on, I've got to get to the store and you to school."

Ten minutes later they went up the lane to the dirt road where they separated. Lilian would wash the dishes, clean the house, and then join Fred at the store before noon.

Jeff headed toward the little wooden schoolhouse a mile away. He carried his arithmetic and speller strapped together. His lunch was in a blue, two-pound lard pail.

The road was a winding pair of foot-deep ruts. This morning they held an inch or so of brown water and soft mud, so Jeff walked on the shoulder until he got to the big flat rock where he always met Hank Alderman.

Jeff sat down to wait. There was no sign of Hank on the side road that ran into this one. But then he was always slow. Hank might make them both late for school but Jeff didn't care.

From where he sat he could see down the gradual slope over the low brush to his home below and to the barn and white fence enclosing their ten acres. It looked toy sized against the far backdrop of green grass and distant mountains. He wondered if the horse had headed for those mountains last night. They were only two or three miles off. They leaned over the valley, rising up and up, blanketed with great stands of timber so thick, he'd heard, the sun never penetrated and the ground stayed dank and slimy with moss. From here they looked dark and forbidding. He knew they were filled with all manner of wild, dangerous animals. He'd heard stories in his father's store and Hank's father's blacksmith shop.

There was the story of the cougar who sat on a woodpile and looked through a kitchen window at a baby in its crib. The mother snatched up the child, ran into the other room, and slammed the door.

One of the local hunters had been trailed all night by a pair of cougars. He described vividly how they'd slunk through the trees like the shadows of death following him and filled the night with blood-curdling yowls.

Another had found a cougar lying on a limb under which he was about to pass. Only a quick, lucky shot saved his life.

There was the brutal story of the cougar-bear fight in which both had been found clawed to ribbons, dead.

There were a lot of bear stories. Harve Sanders had killed twelve one winter and was almost clawed. Jeff had heard nothing about wolves, but such forests must be full of them. He'd seen the picture of the sleigh full of people trying to escape while the wolves leapt at the horses' throats.

That forest was no place to be unless you were a husky trapper and a dead shot like Harve Sanders. So Jeff stuck close to the road at all times.

His parents and he had moved here from Portland almost a year ago. Jeff missed the paved streets, lights, crowds, the huge city stores. They'd come because his mother wanted the calm and quiet of the country. His father wanted his own store where the hunting and fishing was good and there was no competition. Si Campbell, the former owner, had built too much store for the business. Then he'd bought ten acres and added a house and barn. He was head-over-heels in debt. The bank had finally foreclosed. The Hunters had bought it at a bargain. The nearest store was in Springfield, seven miles away.

Jeff wished they'd never come. He didn't like the school, most of the kids, or the country.

Where Jeff waited for Hank, a corner of the Decker land came down to the road. A black colt with a white star on his forehead galloped to the fence, stuck his head over, and nickered. Jeff smiled. He often saved his lunch apple and fed it to the colt on the way home. "Not now," he said to him. "Maybe tonight."

He had coveted the colt from the first time he'd seen him last fall. About three-fourths of the kids rode to school, some riding double and many bareback on their cayuses. The small barn and pasture behind the schoolhouse always held six or eight horses.

If he had his own horse the kids couldn't call him clod-hopper. He'd be on an equal with the best. They'd have to accept him.

The black pony nickered again. Jeff didn't covet him this morning. He was thinking of the big red horse again. He bet not a kid in school, not a man in the valley, probably, had ever seen such a horse. If he rode that horse to school he'd be more important even than Billy Decker and his white pony, Snow Flake, his cowboy boots, silver-buckled belt, and big hat. The kids' eyes would pop if he came riding up on such an animal. Jeff could just see the horse prancing into the yard among the kids, head up, nostrils flared, powerful muscles rippling under the red coat. They wouldn't dare call him clodhopper then.

He was smiling, lost in the dream, when Hank Alderman said, "Hey, you sleepin' with your eyes open or somethin'?"

Hank was two years younger than Jeff. He was what Fred called a towhead. He had a shock of pure white hair that hung down over one eye and a cowlick that stood straight up like a rooster's comb. His brows were white and his eyes so pale blue they seemed to have almost no color.

They walked up the road toward school, Hank on one shoulder, Jeff on the other.

"You hear the storm last night?" Hank asked.

"Sure." Jeff started to talk about the horse, then didn't. To tell Hank would ruin the dream he'd been having.

Hank picked up a rock and fired at a blue jay. The jay flew away. "Get all your homework done?"

"Yeah. You?"

"No," Hank scowled. "Wish we was in the same grade, I could copy yours."

Jeff didn't answer. They walked in silence.

There was a pounding of hooves behind them. Billy Decker on Snow Flake raced up the road and passed between them. There was water in the track on Jeff's side. Before he could think to jump aside the pony plunged into it. A great gob of mud and water hit Jeff in the face and ran down his shirt. Billy looked back laughing and shouting, "Clodhopper! Clodhopper!"

"He done that a purpose," Hank said angrily. "Someday! Someday!" He always made that vague threat when he was angry.

Jeff wiped mud and water from his face and shirt. He thought, someday I will do something.

They were still a hundred yards from school when they heard the bell ring. They began to run.

Jeff and Hank came down the road that afternoon swinging their empty lunch buckets. At the spot where the Decker pasture met the road the black colt stuck his head over the fence and nickered. Jeff took the apple he'd saved from lunch, went to the fence and offered it to the colt. He lifted it daintily, his velvet muzzle barely touching Jeff's outstretched palm. His big teeth crunched down.

Jeff didn't hear Billy Decker ride up. The first he knew was when he was shoved violently and Billy yelled, "Feedin' my colt wormy apples, huh. Go on, clodhopper. Get outa here."

"It wasn't wormy," Jeff shot back. "That was my lunch apple."

"You callin' me a liar?" Billy lowered his head, charged into Jeff and knocked him sprawling. Before Jeff could get up Billy straddled his chest and began pounding him. Jeff tried to fight back but he couldn't punch lying flat on his back with Billy's fists raining blows on him. He covered his face with his arm, but one of Billy's punches got through to his eye.

Hank grabbed Billy's hair and pulled him off backward. Jeff scrambled up. Hank and he faced Billy side by side. Billy glared at them. He couldn't lick both of them. "You keep away from my horse or I'll give you a lickin' like you've never had," he threatened. Then he got on Snow Flake and rode off.

"Someday!" Hank said darkly. "Someday!"

Jeff put a finger to his eye. It felt like it was swelling a little. His mother would notice. He'd have to tell the same story he'd used before.

They hiked on down the road heading for Jasper. Hank would go to his father's blacksmith shop and Jeff to the store where his mother would be helping his father. The telephone line to Springfield ran alongside the road and Jeff noticed it was down again. The line hung to trees, dead snags, and flimsy poles. About half the time it didn't work because a cow or horse had knocked over a pole, or a limb had fallen on the line.

They were still a half mile away when the mournful whoo-ooo whoo-ooo of the Short Line whistles chased each other down the valley. The train went up as far as Oakridge in the morning, dropped off the mail, and returned in the evening. Riley Snodgrass, the engineer, was blowing the whistle to let them know he was passing. Both boys raced down the road to reach a spot where they could see.

There she came, the engine and four coaches, black smoke belching from the stack. They stopped and watched, never tiring of the wonder. Very faintly they heard the rumbling of the wheels, the panting of the engine as the miniature-like train crawled across the valley floor and disappeared behind the timber-shrouded mountains. A final long, thin whistle came roping back to them.

"Gonna ride her someday, sure as shootin'," Hank said. "Gonna go clean to Portland, maybe even further. Just go and go far as the tracks go."

"Then what?" Jeff asked.

"Lay more track and keep on goin'."

Jeff would like to go as far as Portland, away from this valley with its menacing mountains and unfriendly people. For both boys the train held a promise.

Jasper wasn't really a town but it was all the people of the upper valley needed with Springfield only seven miles away. It consisted of Al Alderman's Blacksmith Shop, Hunter's General Merchandise Store, and a dinky little yellow depot about three hundred yards away where the train seldom stopped. The mail sacks were tossed off as the Short Line sped through to Springfield in the morning and picked up on the fly as she returned at night. The store and blacksmith shop were situated on opposite sides of the road that ran along the bank of the swift-flowing Willamette River, which bisected the valley.

The boys went into the blacksmith shop first. There were no horses but the smell of them was there. A blue haze from forge fire drifted through the room and bit at Jeff's nostrils. There was a hot, steamy closeness caused by the fire, the heated iron and the cooling tub. The plank floor was littered with old horseshoe nails, bent and twisted shoes, hoof parings, and various pieces of iron and leather strap. An imposing array of long-handled tongs hung from a rack. A row of various weight hammers leaned against the forge.

Al Alderman was making horseshoes. He grinned at them and went on with his work. He was a huge man wearing a leather apron. The story was told that Alderman had said he could shoe a certain fractious cayuse, then carry it outside if necessary. Looking at his massive shoulders, chest, and post-like arms Jeff believed it.

The blacksmith was not one of the early settlers. He did not belong to any faction of old timers. But he was accepted by everyone because he was the finest blacksmith in the valley. He was independent enough to be a friend of the Hunters, and his son Hank followed suit.

The boys sat side by side on an old buggy seat to watch. Jeff was always fascinated with the making of a horseshoe. First a black length of iron went into the fire. The flames leaped into the push of the bellows. The iron turned cherry red, then Alderman bent and fashioned a perfect shoe with mighty but cunning blows that made the sparks shower and the anvil ring. Jeff caught his breath when the hot shoe was thrust with an explosive hiss into the tub to cool. The finished shoe was added to a peg on the wall, and the process began again.

Alderman was pumping the bellows when he bent down

and looked at Jeff's eye and asked, "What's the other feller look like?"

Jeff mumbled, "I — I ran into the door coming out of school."

Hank looked at Jeff and said nothing.

Alderman nodded, "Doors do have a way of gettin' in front of boys' faces for sure. It's a wonder kids grow up without losin' at least one eye."

"Yes, sir," Jeff said. He watched Al make another shoe, then asked, "I guess you know about every horse in the valley."

"Not every horse." Alderman turned the shoe and squinted at it. "I know a lot of 'em though. I shoe most of 'em." The shoe returned to the fire.

"You heard of anybody losing a horse lately?"

"Can't say that I have. But it's not uncommon for somebody to lose a horse now and then."

"You heard of any strange ones around?"

"How do you mean strange? You got some special horse in mind, Jeff?"

"Yes." Jeff looked into the leaping flames and he could see the horse racing up the lane just as plain. Alderman pumped the bellows and listened to his description.

When he finished the big man shook his head. "There's been no horse like that in the shop. What color was he?"

"With the rain on him he looked sort of black. But when he went under the window I thought he was red."

"He sounds like quite an animal."

"You didn't tell me about him," Hank accused. "When'd you see him?"

"Last night in the storm." Jeff told them about it.

"A scared horse running in a storm like that can look some different," Alderman said.

"I suppose so."

Jeff watched Alderman make two more shoes, then he left and crossed the road to the store.

Fred and Lilian stood in the front window looking out at

the river. Once again there were no customers. They were disappointed in the lack of business. Only about half the people on their side of the river traded with them. The others came in only for their mail. They drove the seven miles to Springfield to shop. At first the Hunters couldn't understand why. Their prices were right, the quality good. Then Harve Sanders, the trapper, stopped at the store one day and summarized a short history of the valley. After supper that night Fred told Lilian and Jeff about it.

"This part of the valley was settled by people who crossed the plains by wagon train seventy years ago. The train became lost. Frank Decker, Lem's father, who'd come out the year before, went back and found them and guided them into this valley where they all settled. Those people never forgot they owed their lives to Decker. Frank became a sort of undeclared kingpin. For years they were a close-knit group living among themselves. They intermarried, cousins marrying cousins, until a good share of the present generation are related. Now it adds up to a sort of big, loosely-knit family, which still looks up to Decker. Lem. It's a crazy situation."

"Why to Lem?"

"He's the wealthiest in the valley. When Frank died he inherited the position."

"The king is dead," Lilian murmured, "long live the king. His enemy is their enemy. And Lem's decided we are the enemy. Is that right?"

"Something like that. Lem and Si Campbell, who owned this store, are cousins. Lem's convinced we teamed up with the bank to rob Campbell of his store. So they're committed to running us out. Their friends and relatives side in with them."

"If we'd only known."

"Now we've got to work at winning these people over," Fred said.

The Hunters invited folks who didn't come or made excuses. They attended dances and were snubbed by half the crowd. Lilian's offer to help at a quilting bee was coolly rejected. Fred brought out several new rifles for the men to try out behind the store. Hundreds of rounds were fired into stumps and trees but trade did not increase.

"What do we do now?" Lilian asked.

"Keep trying," Fred said stubbornly. "Once they get to know us, things will change." That had been months ago.

Lilian saw Jeff crossing the road. She waved and smiled.

Even with things going wrong, his mother tried to remain cheerful, Jeff thought proudly.

Hunter's General Merchandise was big for a country store. There was a huge grocery section with tiers of food-loaded shelves and bins for sugar, salt, flour. There were barrels of crackers and pickles and rounds of yellow cheese half as big as a wagon wheel. There was a hardware section with hammers, saws, nails, and building tools of all kinds. A drug section had hundreds of plain and fancy bottles of patent medicines. On the other side were a harness section, with hames and collars and harnesses hanging from pegs, a shoe section, and a dry goods section with bolts of cloth, yarn, and a thousand kinds of thread. There was even a toy department with dolls, tops, wind-up trains, and erector sets mixed in with rifles, shotguns, and cases of ammunition. The post office took up the back of the store. One whole wall was lined with postal boxes. In the center of all this squatted a huge pot-bellied stove with benches on either side so people could sit and warm themselves.

The moment Jeff came through the door Lilian asked, "What happened to your eye?"

"I ran into the door at school."

"You did that last fall, too."

"I know." He wanted to get off the subject of his eye so he said to his father, "The telephone line's down again between here and home."

"It's been down all day," Fred said. "Maybe they'll send somebody out from Springfield tomorrow to fix it."

A few minutes later Lilian left for home to start supper.

Jeff stayed with his father. He found a toy catalog some drummer had left and sat in back near the post office looking

22

at all the wonderful things for sale. Much of them they had in stock in the store, but they always looked more enticing in the pictures.

A couple of people came in for mail. One woman spent a long time making up her mind about three yards of cloth. Fred was about to begin locking up when Chad Decker, Billy's big brother, and three other young men stopped by. Chad leaned against a counter and looked around the store. He was about twenty, Jeff guessed, and a smaller edition of his big, bruising father. Like Billy, he had a hair-trigger temper. He was dead against the Hunters and talked it up all over the valley. His friends bought Bull Durham tobacco and cigarette papers, then stopped at one of the showcases and looked at the mouth organs. They spent some time trying them out. Finally they bought one and left.

Fred put a pair of work gloves in his pocket and locked up.

When they left the store, Al Alderman and Hank had already gone home. Chad Decker and his friends were strolling off along the riverbank.

The late winter sun had dropped behind the far hills and the red glow of evening was beginning to seep around the edges of the sky. Jeff and Fred started up the road. In the evening silence they heard the sweet music of the mouth organ. Fred stopped and they listened. Whoever was playing was good. Then they heard the singing:

> Down by the old mill stream, where I
>   first met you,
> With your eyes so blue, dressed in ging-
>   ham too.
> It was there I knew, that I loved you true.
> You were sixteen, my village queen,
> Down by the old mill stream.

The sound carried softly on the stillness and Fred Hunter listened, head up, broad lips faintly smiling:

The old mill wheel is silent, and has
    fallen down.
The old oak tree is shattered and lies
    there on the ground. . . .

The sound faded as they apparently went down over the
riverbank. "Pretty," Fred said. "Mighty pretty." He looked
about, drawing a deep breath. The breeze was heavy and fresh
with the scent of fir and of the earth barely stirring with the
last of winter. "Nice here," he said. "You wouldn't hear anything like that in a thousand years in the city."

They went up the road and Fred asked, "Who gave you
the black eye?" When Jeff looked at him startled, he added, "I
don't know why boys use that door excuse. I used it, too. But
when you run into a door your forehead or cheek is bruised.
Yours isn't. Who gave it to you?"

"Billy Decker."

Fred said nothing for a few steps, then, "I thought so.
Did you win?"

"No."

"He gave you the one you got the first day of school,
too?"

"Yes."

"And you lost that one, too?"

"Yes."

"What were those fights about?" When Jeff hesitated
Fred said, "Come on, son. It's no disgrace to get into a slug-
fest now and then. Most boys do. What were they about?"

Jeff told him about the first day of school and the fight
again today. Then the dam broke and the whole miserable
school year came tumbling out.

Fred listened, fists jammed into his pockets, black eyes
beginning to look stormy. When Jeff finished he said, "I'm
sorry. I thought your mother and I were the only ones having
trouble. But apparently they're tarring you with the same
brush."

"Tarring?"

"Just a saying. The bulk of this valley which hangs together like glue is blaming you also because Si Campbell lost his store."

They turned in at their own lane and the sun had dropped beneath the mountains. Half the sky was blood red. Fred said, "Don't say anything about this to Mother. After supper I want you to come out to the barn with me."

"Why?"

"Just come out, that's all."

Supper was ready and they ate in companionable silence. Afterward when Fred got the milk pail and headed for the barn Jeff went along. They let Trixie in, fed her, and then Fred got an empty grain sack and began filling it with straw and punching it down tight. When it was full he hung it from a beam with a length of rope so that it swung about at Jeff's chest. "Now this," he explained, "is a punching bag. Prize fighters use them all the time to develop their speed and punch. Theirs are made of leather and they're not stuffed with straw. But this will suit our purpose."

"You know about prize fighting?" Jeff asked.

"A little. My best friend became a fighter. He wanted me to, but I was going with your mother then and she said no. Guess I should have taught you something about the manly art of self-defense long ago. There's no reason why you can't give Billy a good fight; maybe even lick him. You're about the same size. He's a little heavier, maybe a little stronger. But not too much. What does he do that gets you?"

"He knocks me down and before I can get up he sits straddle of my chest and begins pounding me. I can't roll him off."

"How does he knock you down? Here, do it to me just like he does to you."

Jeff lowered his head and charged into his father's hard middle.

"He did that both times and you let him get away with it?"

"He does it first. I don't know how to stop him."

Fred smiled. "All right, do it again."

Jeff dropped his head and charged. This time his father wasn't there. A foot shot out and he sprawled on his face.

Fred hauled him up explaining, "I sidestepped your charge and tripped you. Very simple. You've got to watch him and keep your wits about you. Think and plan what you're going to do. Don't stand there flat-footed and let him do it."

"Maybe he won't do it next time."

"He did it both times before and got away with it," Fred pointed out. "Of course he will. It's obvious Billy knows nothing about boxing or fighting. I'm going to teach you enough to take care of yourself." He handed Jeff the gloves he'd brought from the store. "Put them on. They're not bag punching gloves but they'll serve the purpose. Now this bag represents your opponent," he explained. "You punch it like you plan to punch him."

"Billy, you mean?"

"Or anybody else. Now, stand up here." He showed Jeff how to place his feet, to hold his hands high in a guarding position. How to snap out his left, then follow with a right. Jeff punched the swinging bag while Fred gave advice, "Keep your head up and your eyes open. Never close your eyes. You can't see where to throw a punch with your eyes shut. Throw that left again. Don't just hit the bag. Figure to drive it back with the punch. That's it. Good! Good! You keep at it while I milk."

It took about ten minutes to milk Trixie. When Fred finished he called a halt. Jeff was panting.

"You think I might lick Billy?" Jeff puffed.

"Practice every night and I think you'll give a good account of yourself. Always remember to keep your head up, your eyes open and try to out-think your opponent all the time." He put the gloves out of sight on a shelf, then took down the sack and tossed it up into the loft. "We've got to keep this to ourselves. Mother doesn't hold with fighting."

"Maybe Billy won't pick on me again."

"If not, fine. Don't start anything. But if you have to fight, wade in and give it all you've got. Now, we'd better get back before Mother comes out to see what's keeping us."

The evening went as always. Jeff did homework under the oil lamp at the dining room table. His father read the paper. His mother sat on the opposite side of the table mending one of the shirts he'd torn yesterday. When Jeff finally finished his homework his mother had mended the shirt and was putting her sewing basket away. His father was on the last page of the paper. It was time for bed.

Jeff climbed the stairs, got into his pajamas, and went to the window for a last look at the night. They sky was clear. The stars were very bright. A fat sickle of moon rode low over the barn roof. He could see the lane, the barn, and the pasture clearly. He thought about the horse. It was beginning to seem a little like a dream. But it had been real. The prints were still down there in the lane. He wondered if he'd ever see the horse again. The way he was running Jeff bet he was clear out of the country by now. He felt a loss he couldn't explain. He climbed into bed and pulled the covers up to his chin. So ended a day in the life of Jeff Hunter in the year 1915.

- 3 -

JEFF'S EYE did not turn black. A slight discoloration showed in the flesh beneath, but it was gone in a few days.

At school Billy Decker asked loudly in front of the other kids, "Hey, clodhopper, what happened to your eye?"

When Jeff pretended not to hear, the kids grinned and snickered.

Jeff searched for the horse along the road and in the brush as he went to and from school each day. In the morning he took a quick look for tracks in the lane.

One night Jeff awoke to the sound of rain on the road and wind whistling through the big bare maple limbs. He jumped out of bed and ran to the window. Maybe the horse had returned and was again trying to get into the dry barn. He crouched there, straining his eyes into the night until he was shivering with cold. But no horse came. The horse was gone for good. He'd never see him again. He was almost ready to believe he'd dreamed it all.

Every night the straw-filled punching sack was swung from the timber in the barn. Fred milked by lantern light while Jeff punched the sack. From time to time Fred glanced up and called out advice, "Keep those hands high. Keep that left snapping out there. Step around the bag. Don't stay nailed to the floor. Move! Move!" When the milking was done the sack was returned to the loft and the gloves hidden on the shelf.

After milking one night Fred said, "You're doing pretty fair. Let's see how good you really are." He crouched in front of Jeff. "Let's see you hit me. Come on, I'm the punching bag."

"You mean, really try?" Jeff asked.

"Of course. Come on. Let go with all you've got. Let's see what you've learned."

Jeff stepped around his father looking for an opening. His father's hands were so big Jeff could hardly find a spot to throw a punch. He tried swinging one around the hands but it was deftly pushed aside. He tried a jab that was caught in Fred's big palm. He tried another and then a right. Both punches were caught. Then his face was lightly cuffed by both right and left. Jeff kept moving around, throwing punches, trying to find an opening. Fred kept cuffing his face and picking off the punches. Then Jeff noticed a hole between his father's elbows. He threw a left that was caught in Fred's palm like a baseball. He brought his right up from underneath into the hole. His fist smacked solidly on the end of his father's nose. The blood flew.

Jeff dropped his hands, aghast.

Fred rubbed a hand across his nose, looked at the streak of blood, and laughed, "I'll be darned. Hey, you really pack a punch!"

"I'm sorry," Jeff stammered. "I didn't mean to."

"The heck you didn't," Fred said. "I told you to try to hit me and you did. I got careless and left an opening. You found it. You used your head and I made a mistake. That's what wins fights." He slapped Jeff on the shoulder. "I've got to stop this bleeding before we go to the house."

He went to the water trough and washed his face for several minutes before the bleeding stopped. Then they hurriedly put the punching sack in the loft, hid the gloves, and headed for the house. As they walked into the kitchen Fred's nose began bleeding again.

Lilian got a basin of water and a towel and stood watching. She smiled faintly as he stemmed the flow.

"Did you run into a door, too?" she asked.

"What?" Fred turned holding the wet towel to his nose.

"You and Jeff actually had me believing that 'running

into a door' business for a while. Did you put Jeff's punching sack back in the loft? Oh yes, and hide the gloves on the shelf?"

Jeff and Fred just stared at her.

Lilian folded her arms and said, "I got suspicious when you went to the barn together every night. It took too long to milk. Then I began putting two and two together. Jeff's getting a pretty good punch, isn't he?"

"You saw it?"

"Through a crack."

"You've been spying on us every night," Fred accused.

"Oh, I missed a few," she smiled.

Fred wiped his nose again and looked at Jeff, "Your mother is a very smart woman."

"Jeff's getting pretty good, isn't he?" Lilian asked.

"You saw how good. Any objections?"

Lilian bit her lips, "Billy gave you that black eye the first day of school, didn't he?"

"Yes," Jeff said.

"Does Mr. Jacoby know?"

"Yes."

"What did he say to Billy?"

"That he ought to be ashamed."

"That's all?"

"Yes."

"Maybe it's time someone talked with Mr. Jacoby."

"That would make it tougher on Jeff," Fred said. "It'd look like he was hiding behind his mother. Let the boys take care of this themselves. Jacoby's handling it right."

"And let Jeff get beat up again?"

"He hasn't been hurt. And maybe, if there's a next time, he'll win. That's what this practice has been all about. Believe me, Lil, this is the best way for Jeff. Let the kids settle their own problems. Then the air will be cleared. No outsiders can do it for them, any more than they could settle our problems. We're going to have to do that."

"I don't like Jeff being dragged into our feud, or whatever you call it," Lilian said. "But I should have known he would be." For the first time she looked discouraged, "Maybe we should admit we're licked and get out."

"Not yet," Fred said stubbornly. "I'm not licked by a long shot."

Later, doing homework at the dining room table Jeff heard his parents in the kitchen. Lilian asked, "You really think Jeff might beat Billy Decker in a fight?"

"Punching a sack of straw is one thing," Fred said. "Trying to hit another fellow who's also trying to hit you is something else. It'll depend entirely on Jeff."

Jeff did not sleep well that night. Maybe it was the excitement of having bloodied his father's nose or knowing his mother found them out. He lay in bed and watched a full moon crawl a pattern across the wall. He thought of the horse, and Billy, and the store troubles. He was dropping off to sleep when he became aware that he'd been hearing a steady sound for several minutes. He listened carefully. The corral gate was rattling a little.

He smiled. Trixie had an itch and was using it for a rubbing post. Then he remembered Trixie was in the barn. He jumped out of bed and ran to the window. In the soft light of the full moon he could see almost as plain as day. A horse stood at the gate, its head over the top bar looking toward the barn. The sound he'd heard was its pawing at the gate to get in.

Jeff took the stairs two at a time, raced down the dark hall to his parents' bedroom and whispered harshly, "Dad! Dad! He's here. The horse is here!"

"Huh?" Fred mumbled sleepily. "Horse? What horse?"

"The horse, Dad. He's come back! He's at the pasture gate now trying to get in."

"Oh, that horse. The cayuse." Fred sat up with maddening deliberation and reached for a robe. Lilian was getting up on the other side.

"Hurry!" Jeff whispered. "Before he leaves. Hurry up!"

"Some bony local cayuse and I'm supposed to get all excited and break my neck getting out there to see him," Fred grumbled.

With Jeff leading the way they hurried down the hall into the kitchen. Jeff quietly opened the door and stepped outside. Fred followed.

The horse was plainly visible. He stood pawing at the gate. Jeff could even see the big hoof hitting the bottom pole. Behind them Lilian let the kitchen door slam. Instantly the horse whirled and plunged up the lane, head up, mane flying, legs driving. He thundered past them, crossed the road, and disappeared into the night.

They listened to the pound of his hooves die away and Lilian said, "Good heavens, what an animal! I'm sorry I let the door slam and frightened him off."

"We couldn't have got near him anyway," Fred said. "He's sure spooky. But Jeff's right about one thing, he's no cayuse."

Jeff was shaking. His mouth was dry, "What — what kind of horse is he, Dad?"

Fred shook his head, "I'm no expert on horses. But he looks like some kind of special horse. And don't ask me what I mean by that. I've never seen his like around here. If he belongs to anybody in the valley it'll be Lem Decker. He's got some mighty fine horses."

They went inside and Lilian lit the lamp. "What're you going to do about him, Dad?" Jeff asked.

"Do?" Fred squinted at his son. "Nothing for me to do. I'm going to tell Lem about him when he comes in for the mail, which should be about tomorrow. If the animal's not his, maybe he'll know who he does belong to. It's up to Lem or whoever owns the horse to do something about him. Not me." He yawned hugely, "Guess I'll go back to bed. Excitement seems to be over."

Next morning Jeff was bursting to tell Hank about the horse's visit.

"Nothin' to get all excited about," Hank said calmly. "Like your pa said, he's likely Lem's."

"Suppose he isn't," Jeff said hopefully.

"Bet he is." Hank shied a rock at a bird and watched it fly away. "Pa says he's got some awful good horses. That big Blackie of his is the fastest horse around. But what do you care? You sound like you want that horse for your own self."

Jeff had never admitted it aloud. He did now. "I do," he said.

"Fat chance," Hank said. "Lem Decker don't give up anything. Pa says he's tighter'n the bark on a tree. That's how come he's the richest man in the valley. Anyhow, you said your folks wouldn't let you have a horse."

"I know."

"How'd you figure to catch him, for gosh sakes?" Hank asked.

"I don't know."

There was a clatter of hooves behind them and they jumped out of the road. Billy Decker raced by on Snow Flake, tossing a derisive, "You're gonna be late, clodhopper. Clodhopper."

"Someday," Hank warned. "Just wait. Someday." But Billy was right. They began to hurry.

The first thing Jeff asked when he entered the store that night was, "Is it Lem Decker's horse, Dad?"

"Lem says it's possible. He lost one some months ago and never found him. He's coming by tomorrow morning to pick up his track at our place and try to run him down."

Jeff made a secret wish that Lem would not find the horse, and if he did, that he wouldn't catch him.

The next day was Saturday. Jeff stayed home when both his parents left for the store. He wanted to be there when Lem Decker came to take up the horse's tracks from their lane.

When Lem finally arrived he was not alone. Chad, Billy, and two neighbors, Johnny Walsh and Benny Wallace, were along. They stopped in front of the house and Lem called to Jeff. "Where'd he cross the road boy?"

Lem Decker was a big, scowling, burly looking farmer who seldom smiled. He had dark, coarse features and a rough, pock-pitted skin. His manner was overbearing and demanding. Lem was riding Blackie, a big powerful looking animal. It was generally agreed that he was the fastest horse in the valley. He was Lem's pride and joy. Jeff had seen Blackie from a distance but not close up till now. He was as big as the red horse. His legs were long and slender. He had the same head-high, ears-forward look. Except for color, the two horses were much alike.

"Boy!" Lem was impatient. "I asked you a question."

Jeff pointed to the tracks still visible in the soft earth, "He crossed here and went that way, up toward the mountains."

Lem looked in the direction the tracks went, then around at the country.

Benny Wallace smiled at Jeff, "You comin' along?" Benny's family was one of the old timers in the valley, but Benny didn't let Lem dictate to him. He traded at the store and was friendly.

"I haven't any horse," Jeff said.

"Couldn't ride it, if you did," Billy snorted.

Jeff ignored him and asked Benny, "Do you think you'll find him?"

"I think so. The ground's soft. His tracks won't be hard to follow."

"We'll catch 'im, too," Billy said. "Wait till Blackie gets on his tail."

Chad asked, "You think it might be old Mike, Pa?"

"No tellin'. My guess is he's up around Buttercup Canyon. It's a good place for a loose horse to hang out. There's plenty of grass and shelter from storms."

"He could of turned off and headed for them bare buttes," Chad suggested.

Lem scowled at his son and said, "Buttercup Canyon." He rode off. The rest fell in behind.

Jeff watched them out of sight. Again he made his wish that if they found the horse, they wouldn't catch him.

Jeff puttered around the house and kept watching in the direction of Buttercup Canyon for their return. It was late

34

afternoon when the five riders emerged from the brush and entered the road. They did not have the big red horse. Their own mounts looked beat. The men slumped in the saddle.

Jeff ran up the lane and asked, "Did you find him?"

Lem Decker just looked at Jeff. He didn't bother to answer.

Benny Wallace said tiredly, "We found him all right, about where Lem figured. That red brute led us a merry chase all day. Nobody got close enough to even toss a rope in his direction. He played with us. He ran our horses right off their legs."

"Blackie, too?" Jeff felt a rush of relief.

Bennie nodded. "That animal don't run, he flies. Every time we thought we had him in a pocket, he turned on speed and simply ran away from us. We finally lost him in the timber. Never did see him again."

"Blackie didn't get a fair shake," Chad pointed out. "He was packin' Pa. The red was runnin' light."

"Wouldn't have mattered," Johnny Walsh said. "There were five of us. We pulled every trick we know to corner him and couldn't. He's not only fast, he's leary of a man on horseback. That horse has been run before and knows what to expect. I've a feeling a man on foot carrying a bucket of oats might have the best chance of getting close to him."

"Maybe," Benny agreed. "He's been around people because he's shod."

Jeff trotted alongside the tired cavalcade and said, "Then he isn't yours, Mr. Decker?"

"No," Lem muttered.

"Will you go after him again?"

"Boy, you talk too much," Lem said annoyed.

"We have to," Johnny Walsh said. "Can't let a stallion run loose."

"Why?"

"Gee, are you dumb, clodhopper," Billy sneered. "Don't you know anything?"

"He's a stallion," Benny explained to Jeff. "And like all

stallions he'll start raiding ranches to steal mares to make his own band. We can't afford to lose horses. So we've got to catch him or drive him out of the valley."

"Or shoot 'im," Billy said.

Benny nodded, "Even that."

"You can't!" Jeff was shocked. "He belongs to somebody."

"We can, if it becomes necessary," Benny said. "Course he ain't raided any ranches yet. But it's a mortal cinch he's gonna want his own band. But shootin' is the last thing, of course. Nobody want to do that. We'd rather catch him or run him out. But something will have to be done about him if he keeps hanging around this valley. It's plain that fellow spells nothing but trouble. Whoever he belongs to is responsible for what happens to him. Not us."

"When will you go after him again?" Jeff asked fearfully.

"In a couple of days maybe. He's spooky as all get out, after the way we ran him today. We'll let him settle down again. Maybe we can figure some way to get close enough to dab a rope on 'im."

Jeff stopped in the road and watched them ride on. One way or another they meant to get the big horse, and they didn't sound too confident about running him down and capturing him. That meant just one thing to Jeff. Lem would shoot the horse with no more regret than killing a rabbit. He returned to the house worried and depressed at the thought of men hunting the horse like some wild animal. Then he remembered that Johnny Walsh had said the horse was leary of a mounted man and that someone on foot with a bucket of oats might have a better chance of getting close to him because he'd been around people.

Jeff sat down in the kitchen thinking and finally an idea crawled into his mind like a snake into a bush. It seemed a little crazy, but he had a boy's enthusiasm and concern, also a complete ignorance of horses. He needed Hank's help, Jeff decided, to show him where Buttercup Canyon was. And more important he wanted Hank along because he was afraid to go into those forbidding mountains alone. At church tomorrow, he decided, he'd try to enlist Hank.

Getting dressed for church was a chore Jeff hated. He had to polish and wear his button shoes, a white blouse and tie, knickers and long black stockings. Fred wore his suit, overcoat, and black derby hat. Lilian wore the special white shawl she had knitted years before. She wore it only on special occasions like going to church, to a party, or when they went visiting.

The three waited until the Aldermans came by in their two-seater buggy to pick them up. Al, his buxom wife, Ellie, and Hank all rode in the front seat leaving the back for the three Hunters.

The church was a little white, wooden building which seated seventy or eighty people. It was about two-thirds full. The Aldermans and Hunters sat in the back row. For this day Hank wore clean overalls, a white shirt, and had his white hair slicked down with water. The cowlick still stood stiffly erect.

The boys were separated by their parents but they could peek around and grin at each other. The big wood stove up front began to throw out heat and a couple of flies started buzzing against the windowpane. Both boys watched until Fred poked Jeff in the ribs with his elbow. Al punched Hank so vigorously it brought forth an audible grunt and annoyed frowns from several near people.

Reverend Callison droned on and on. Jeff became sleepy. His head began to droop. This brought another punch from Fred. Finally the last hymn was sung and the people filed outside and scattered to buggies and wagons. Cora Decker smiled at Lilian and might have spoken, but Lem hurried her to the surrey.

Lem and his wife sat in the front seat, Chad and Billy behind them. Billy saw Jeff and held his nose with his fingers and twisted up his face. Jeff watched them drive off, the patent leather of the surrey gleaming, the fringe ringing, the top swinging, the horses stepping out. There was no doubt the Deckers were what Fred called "upper-crust."

Jeff got Hank to one side and asked, "You know where Buttercup Canyon is?"

"About three miles from your place. There must be a million buttercups there in the summer. Why?"

"You want to go up there with me this afternoon?"

"Heck, no. I've been there lots of times." Hank looked at Jeff suspiciously, "What you wanta go up there for anyway?"

"There's something mighty special up there," Jeff said mysteriously. Hank loved mysteries and by pretending one Jeff figured he couldn't resist.

"For gosh sakes, this's Sunday," Hank said.

"This's more important than any Sunday."

"What's so important about Buttercup Canyon? It's just a big hole in the mountains."

"That's what you think."

"That's what I know."

"It's not the canyon. It's what's up there that's special."

"All right. What's there?"

"I can't tell you. But nobody else knows. Nobody," Jeff added. "You'll see when we get up there."

"What'll I see?"

"Come with me and find out. You won't be sorry."

"Yeah, I'll bet."

"You won't. That's a promise."

Still Hank hesitated.

"It's so special I can't even tell my folks," Jeff said as a clincher.

That decided Hank. "Well, all right. Where'll we meet?"

"That big rock across the road and straight out from our place, right after we eat. And don't tell anybody else."

"Don't worry, I wouldn't dare."

Fred Hunter called, "Let's go, boys." The grownups were already in the buggy.

Jeff could hardly wait until dinner was over. He changed clothes, sneaked out to the barn, wound a halter and rope around his body under his coat and tied it. He got a small bucket of oats, held it under his coat, out of sight, and wandered up the lane, crossed the road, and vanished into the brush.

The rock was about a quarter of a mile from the road. It was as far as Jeff had ever been alone. He took the pail of oats from under his coat, unwound the rope and halter, and sat down to wait for Hank.

Hank arrived a few minutes later and said, "Hey! What's the halter and bucket of oats for? A horse?"

"Yes."

"That's what's so special!" Hank said angrily. "A horse! For gosh sakes. Just a dumb horse."

"Not a dumb horse. It's the one I've been telling you about for a week."

"A dumb horse. You fooled me. I got a notion not to go."

"You promised," Jeff reminded him.

"And you promised something special. What's so special about this horse, anyway?"

Jeff told him how Lem Decker with the help of four men had tried to catch the horse.

"He ran away from Lem's Blackie? I can't hardly believe that. Blackie's the fastest in the valley."

"Benny says he don't run. He flies."

He's still just a horse," Hank insisted. "Pa shoes 'em every day."

"You haven't seen this horse."

"Seen plenty of others."

"You're here now," Jeff coaxed. "Come with me."

"What's the matter?" Hank asked shrewdly. "You scared to go up to Buttercup Canyon alone?"

"I've never been there."

"You can't miss it."

"You've got nothing else to do. You might as well come along."

Hank considered. "Well, all right. But I wouldn't of if I'd known it was just an old horse."

They started off but Hank wasn't through complaining yet. "What's the halter and bucket of oats for? You figure to catch him on foot when Lem's big Blackie and four men couldn't? You figure to just walk up to him easy as pie?"

"They've been running him," Jeff explained. "Johnny Walsh says he's afraid of men on horses. Maybe that's why he's hard to catch. Maybe he's always been around people on foot. Maybe somebody walking, taking his time, and not running him, he'll understand and not be afraid of."

"Maybe, maybe," Hank mimicked. "You're full of maybes! You sure are a city kid. You don't know a thing about horses. If Pa heard this he'd bust a stitch laughing. You're crazy as a loon. No wonder you're scared to tell your folks. Your pa'd likely tan your hide."

Jeff said nothing. They walked in silence. Finally Hank asked, "You figure he hangs out in Buttercup Canyon?"

"That's where they found him and where they lost him."

It took almost an hour to hike there, and it began to drizzle. They were soaked halfway to the knees. They were following a pair of old wagon tracks so thickly grown over with grass they were mere shadows on the land. Jeff asked, "I didn't know there used to be a road here."

"Didn't. This's where that wagon train of people came down into the valley a long time ago."

"You mean the lost wagon train Lem's father hunted up?"

"Sure. Lem told Pa that some of them even had cows hitched to their wagons cause the horses had died. And some had a cow and a horse hitched up together. I guess they were a real sorry sight."

For a moment Jeff forgot about the big red horse as he thought of these people who'd come dragging into the valley more dead than alive, and he understood a little how they could continue to stick closely together and a Decker still be a kingpin after all these years.

They came to the heavy timber and Jeff asked nervously, "You think we might see a cougar or bear or something?"

"Naw, bears are still sleepin' and cougars come out mostly at night."

"What'll we do if we see one?"

40

"For gosh sakes, we ain't seen one yet. If you're so scared why'd you come?"

"I'm not exactly scared — much."

"Then quit actin' like it."

Buttercup Canyon was a big, flat meadow with steep canyon walls rising on either side. It narrowed to a funnel at the far end that punched into a high ridge. A small stream came down the center of the meadow with brush growing along either bank. The grass of the canyon floor was long, green, and thick. The ground was spongy from the winter rains. A few early buttercups lifted yellow heads through the grass. The area was empty of life.

"We had this whole hike for nothin'," Hank grumbled. "Just like I figured. There ain't even a bird here in winter."

"This is where they found him," Jeff insisted. He pointed to a maze of hoof prints. "There, see."

"Sure," Hank said. "From the gang that chased him. They probably run him clean outa the country. Up that far end where it narrows down, it cuts through the high ridge and goes into another big valley on the other side. I'll bet that's where your old horse is. I ain't goin' no farther. I gotta get home or I'll catch it."

Jeff looked around. He guessed his idea had been pretty foolish. "All right, we'll go back." He was turning to leave when he caught a flash of movement in the brush bordering the creek. The horse came up the bank and stood looking at them no more than fifty yards away. It was the first daylight look Jeff had of him and his breath caught in his throat. "Hank, there!" he whispered. "There!"

The horse stood head up, sharp ears pricked forward, nostrils flared as if he searched the slight breeze for some scent of them. Even at this distance Jeff could feel that every muscle was tuned to whirl and spring away. To Jeff he was like a leaping flame. He was thundering hooves shattering the silence of a moonlight night. He was a breath-catching glimpse of speed and plunging power in a blinding flash of rain-streaked lightning.

Then Hank said, "Well, there's your old horse. Let's see

you walk up to 'im."

Jeff started to walk forward slowly, his heart hammering. He held out the bucket of oats and began to talk to the horse. "Come on," he tipped the bucket so the horse could see inside. "You know what this is. Come and get it. I'm not going to hurt you. Come on, boy. Come on."

The horse's ears jumped nervously back and forth as he listened. He pawed the ground and tossed his head impatiently. Jeff thought he was going to whirl and dash away. He stopped. He shook the bucket of oats and kept talking, softly, coaxingly, "You know what these are. Oats, boy. Oats."

The horse nickered and to Jeff's utter amazement began coming slowly toward him a step at a time. It seemed to Jeff he got bigger and bigger. They boy's throat was suddenly dry. He couldn't talk. He just stood there and held out the bucket of oats invitingly, and waited. Step by slow, careful step the animal drew near. Jeff heard the breath rushing through his nostrils. He smelled the warm steam of his rain-wet coat. His eyes were big and clear. He looked wary. He stopped in front of Jeff and stretched his neck. Eager lips reached for the bucket. Jeff started to put out his hand to touch him when with startling suddenness he whirled and was off. He leaped down the creek bank, raced through the water, and lunged up the opposite bank. He dashed across the open and disappeared into the heavy timber. Jeff looked after him feeling a little sick.

Hank came up beside him and said, "Well, he's gone. No use of us hanging around here. Come on, let's go home. I'm gettin' wet."

"What scared him?"

"Who knows what scares a horse. He got scared, that's all. That horse is half wild. Maybe he came up to you because you looked and acted different and he was curious. Then when he smelled you he knew it was man smell and took off."

"I almost had him," Jeff said. "I could almost touch him."

"Well, you ain't got him now," Hank said. "And the way he took off he ain't comin' back. Come on, let's go home."

Jeff put the bucket of oats on the ground in a clear spot

where it could be seen. "Maybe he'll come back for it." He turned reluctantly and followed Hank back out of the canyon. He said finally, "He sure can run, can't he?"

"Sure," Hank said, "all horses can run."

"But not like him. You said yourself that Blackie was the fastest horse in the valley. Well, Benny Wallace said this one ran him right off his legs." Jeff was determined Hank should be impressed with the big red horse.

"All right, he can run," Hank agreed. "What difference does it make if he runs fast or slow? He's just another horse."

Jeff didn't answer. Hank would never understand how he felt.

- 4 -

THEY WERE EATING dinner Tuesday evening when Fred said, "Check Wallace was in this morning. He said the red stallion was up at his place last night trying to steal a couple of his mares."

"What do you mean 'steal'?" Jeff asked.

"Just that. He's a stallion, and he wants his own band. When he sees a mare he wants he goes after her. If he has to bust down fences or fight another stallion for her, he does. Check said he heard a terrific racket out by the barn and when he got there the red stallion was kicking his corral to pieces to get at the mares. When Check showed up he took off like a bullet. There's going to be trouble with that fellow loose."

"Maybe it was some other stallion that looks like him," Jeff said hopefully.

Fred shook his head. "It was him all right."

The next night it happened at Lem Decker's. Johnny Walsh brought the news to the store. The big stallion had broken through the pasture fence at Decker's and made off with two of Lem's mares. Lem was mad. He was organizing a hunt to go after the horse the next day to kill him.

"They can't do that," Jeff cried. "He belongs to somebody. He's not a wild horse."

"You can't call him tame when nobody can catch him. He's breaking down fences and stealing mares right out of corrals and pastures. You're right, Jeff, he does belong to someone. Trouble is nobody knows who, and the damage he's causing makes him free game. Ranchers don't have to put up with his depredations. Killing seems about the only sure way of stopping him."

"There ought to be some way to catch him," Jeff insisted.

"There probably is, but it could take weeks. The big fellow's fast, smart, and cagey. These ranchers don't have the time it'd take to run him down, and they don't feel he's worth the effort. To them he's a menace, and an outlaw."

"It seems a shame to shoot that beautiful animal just because they can't catch him," Lilian said.

"Sure," Fred agreed. "But the ranchers don't want to lose any more stock. I don't blame them."

"Can't they run him out of the country?" Lilian asked.

"He'd come back. Once a stallion sets his mind on some mares he'll come back, so they tell me."

"Can't you do something?" Jeff begged. "Can't you stop them, Dad?"

"Me?" Fred's black brows came up. "I'm a storekeeper. There's nothing I could do. These ranchers are mad and they're taking the only way out that makes sense to them. Anyway, this is none of our business. I've got plenty of troubles trying to run a store. I learned a long time ago that when you're in business, keep out of the local problems. Lem Decker is Mr. Big in the valley and he's decided to hunt down the horse and do away with him. There isn't a rancher that won't agree with him."

Jeff didn't go to the barn that night to punch the straw sack while Fred milked. Later, when he did his homework he sat toying with the pencil, not even looking at the book. His thoughts were up in Buttercup Canyon.

His mother asked, "Are you stuck, Jeff? Do you want some help?"

"No," he said. He finally settled down to work, finished, and went up to bed. He lay staring at the dark ceiling and thought about the horse, and Lem Decker, and the men who'd go out hunting him tomorrow. It wouldn't be hard to find the horse. He'd be in Buttercup Canyon again. And he'd be in no hurry to run away at sight of the mounted men. He knew with his speed he could easily leave all of them behind. He wouldn't know about the rifles until it was too late. Jeff could even visualize the shock and surprise on his big face as the life was smashed out of him.

Jeff was particularly quiet at breakfast the next morning and Lilian asked, "Aren't you feeling well?"

"I'm all right," he said.

"Then eat your mush. You've hardly touched it."

Fred asked shrewdly, "Still thinking about the horse?" And when Jeff looked up, "I would, too, at your age."

"I don't see why they have to shoot him. If they tried hard enough they could catch him." He almost added, "I walked up to him so close I almost touched him," but he didn't.

"They probably could," Fred agreed. "But there are other things to consider. These people are ranchers, and spring is almost here. They're getting ready now to begin plowing and disking and planting crops. Once spring breaks they'll be working from daylight till dark. Everything has to be ready to go without breakdowns. They're doing that repair work now. They haven't time to spend maybe weeks chasing down a horse that, once captured, may be of little value to them. Obviously he's no farm animal to pull a plow or heavy wagon. He's no draft horse. And maybe at his age, he couldn't be trained for much. There's too many things against trying to catch him and not enough for. It's as simple as that."

"If they all got together and went after him," Jeff insisted. "It wouldn't take long."

"You'd never get them all together. And most of these people don't have topflight saddle horses. That's what it'd take to catch him. Apparently Lem's Blackie is the only one around that can give him a real run. There's no other way, son. I have to agree with Lem on this."

"I don't like killing him," Jeff insisted.

"Sometimes it can't be helped. I'm sure Lem would rather catch him. He appreciates a fast horse. That's why he's got Blackie. But where ranching and animals are concerned unpleasant things sometimes happen. This is one of them. You do what you have to do and go on."

Jeff was slow getting ready for school so Fred went off ahead of him. When he finally went up the lane carrying lunch pail and books he was still thinking about the injustice the local men had planned against the big horse. He thought of Sunday up in Buttercup Canyon; how the horse had walked right up to him, then became frightened and ran.

A thought crept into his mind and he immediately tried to reject it. But it stayed and grew. The more he thought about it the more logical it became.

Out of sight of the house he stopped in the road and stared off toward Buttercup Canyon. He could hike there and find the horse. He couldn't catch him without the halter but he could chase him through the funnel end of the canyon into the next valley where he'd be safe from Lem Decker and the ranchers' guns. It would take a couple of hours and he couldn't get to school before recess. He'd have to do this alone. Hank would never go along. He was a little worried about going up there alone, but he hadn't seen any dangerous wild animals Sunday. Of course Mr. Jacoby and his parents would have to know why he'd been late to school. There'd be punishment, but he refused to think about that. The important thing was he'd be saving the horse's life for a while, anyway.

He turned off the road and began running through the brush toward Buttercup Canyon.

He was panting and tired when he finally came out of the brush and trees onto the canyon floor. He stood a minute looking about, catching his breath.

Then he saw Lem Decker's two mares and the big red horse across the creek. He walked toward them, his heart hammering. He was halfway to the creek when the stallion threw up his head and looked at him. The mares raised their heads for a few curious seconds then resumed eating. The stallion continued to watch him.

Jeff walked straight toward him. He wanted to get as

close as possible before he began shouting and waving his arms. He wanted to scare the horse bad.

Jeff reached the creek, waded across, and climbed the opposite bank. When he broke out of the creek brush the horse was not more than a hundred yards away.

Jeff stopped. The horse was getting nervous. He stamped his front feet and tossed his head and snorted. He walked a few steps toward Jeff. The boy had the odd sensation the big animal was sizing him up, trying to decide whether to run or to stand fast.

Jeff slowly advanced a few more yards. Then suddenly he let out the wildest yell he could summon, leaped into the air, and waved his arms wildly.

Instantly the stallion whirled, rounded up the mares in the twinkling of an eye, and started driving them pell-mell up the narrow end of the canyon. Jeff ran after them waving his arms and shouting. The horses dashed into the heavy timber and brush where the canyon narrowed. They were lost to sight.

Jeff stopped at the timber edge and looked in under the trees. Hank and he hadn't been this far Sunday. It was half dark in there. The thick trees and low limb growth cut off the light and gave it a gloomy look. Sleazy fog banners drifted like ghosts among the limbs and brush. Heavy dew dripped off the limbs. There were big bog holes filled with green looking swamp water. The smell of dead and rotting vegetation rose from the earth. Rank growth and dead and dying trees were all about. It was the spookiest place he'd ever seen. His first reaction was to turn and run. But he could not turn back. He had a job to do.

Jeff ventured in under the trees following the faint marks of the ancient wagon road. The earth turned soft and spongy. Dirty water began to ooze up around his shoe tops. He discovered the thick grass hummocks that grew everywhere would support his weight. He began leaping from hummock to hummock as he progressed deeper into the boggy area.

He came up with the horses again. He shouted and

waved his arms and they went thundering out of sight. They were following the course of the creek through this narrow-walled canyon. They were not going to try to climb the high ridge but were taking the easy way and were cutting straight through into the next valley.

He raised the horses twice more and sent them scampering ahead of him. Each time they ran only a couple hundred yards and he'd find the mares browsing. The stallion was always on the lookout for him.

The ground turned mushy. The grass hummocks no longer supported him. He backed out, circled around, found solid ground and went on. The horses had plunged straight through leaving black holes where their feet sank in. The brush became more dense. He could see no more than thirty or forty feet ahead.

He came on the mares suddenly. They stood together in a tiny clearing and watched him slowly approach as any tame horses would. Then he saw the stallion. The mares had apparently followed the solid ground, and in an attempt to head them off the big horse had plunged recklessly through the boggy spot and was now mired belly deep in the black ooze. He was held tight. His struggle only sank him an inch or so deeper. Jeff knew immediately that the horse was not going to get out of here without a lot of help.

Several inches of clear water, a backup from the creek, flowed over this treacherous bog where the horse was trapped. Jeff put his books and lunch bucket on the ground and began to wade toward the horse. He didn't know what he was gong to do. He just wanted to get out there, touch him, soothe him, take that wild, terrified look from his eyes. He kept saying softly, "Whoa, boy! Easy, boy! Whoa. Whoa."

Ten feet from the horse the black muck gripped Jeff's feet and began to suck him down. In panic he floundered back to solid earth. Now he understood the terror he saw in the horse's eyes and a great sympathy welled up in him for the trapped stallion. He stood there trying to think what to do. The horse lunged upward again and trashed about, but he only sank a little deeper.

Jeff said in his most soothing voice, "Easy, boy! Easy." The horse turned his head and looked at the boy. Then he heaved a great sigh and became still.

Jeff studied the situation. The horse was hopelessly mired and his struggles only drove him deeper. He was going to die in the black ooze unless Jeff could find a way to help him. He thought of running to the store to get his father. But that was almost four miles away. It would be a couple of hours before they could get here. If he left, the horse might continue to thrash around until he sank from sight. He had to stay. He had scared the horse into this. Now he had to find some way to get him out.

The first thing was to get to the animal.

Jeff began hunting for dead limbs. He packed them tightly together in the treacherous muck, building a road to the horse. When he ran out of dead limbs he broke off small ones from the surrounding trees and brush and packed that onto the muck. He got down on his stomach, to distribute his weight, and pushed brush ahead of him as he wriggled his way to the end of his road. The two mares wandered about, a few feet off on solid ground, as though waiting for him to free the stallion.

Jeff kept talking to the horse as he worked, keeping his voice low and soft and intimate. "I saw you that first time in the storm when you came to our barn. Remember? And I saw you there a second time. Is there something about the barn that draws you? Do you remember one like it from another time? Where did you come from anyway? You've got to quit stealing mares. I don't want you killed. I want you for my own. I have from the first night I saw you."

A lot of things he said didn't make sense. But the sound of his voice seemed to keep the horse quiet. As long as Jeff talked to him the sharp ears were up. He turned his head as though watching the boy and listening. Almost, Jeff thought, as if he understood.

Jeff finally reached the horse. He stretched out his hand

and laid it on the smooth arched neck. A prickly thrill went through him. His voice was choked. The words hardly came at all, "Easy, boy, easy. I'm going to get you out of here. Just don't try to move around. Every time you do you sink lower. Lie still, boy! Lie real still!"

He broke off more limbs, crawled out with them and began building a thick mat around the horse's head. If he could build a thick enough mat around those front legs maybe the horse could get his hooves on top of it and lift himself out. Jeff was almost ready to try when he heard a heavy voice call, "Look through that brush over there on your right."

Lem Decker was here! Right in this narrow canyon and coming toward them.

The mares lifted their heads and pricked up their ears. Since he'd found the stallion Jeff had completely forgot about Lem and his death hunt. He crawled out, grabbed the stallion's head and clamped his hand over his nose so he couldn't neigh.

But one of the mares whinnied.

Immediately Lem shouted, "Over here! This way!"

Jeff grabbed up a stick and hurled it at the mare, striking her in the side. Both mares went pelting away through the brush. Chad's voice shouted, "Over here, Pa! They're takin' off straight ahead of me."

Jeff crouched over the stallion's head, held his nose and waited. He recognized Benny Wallace's voice, then Chad's and Johnny Walsh's. Lem's booming voice was urging them on. Horses hooves pounded through the near brush. There was the snap and crack of limbs. He got one flashing glimpse of a big black horse and Lem bent forward looking straight ahead, his rifle swinging from one hand. They all thundered by chasing the two mares.

Jeff waited until the sounds faded away. Then he crawled around in front of the horse. "They'll be back," he warned. "We've got to get you out of here." Swiftly he worked armloads of brush down around the front legs, making a thick mat that he hoped would hold the horse's weight. He tried to dig the black muck away so he could lift the legs and put them on the mat, to give the horse more lifting leverage. But the muck seeped back as fast as he dug. He'd have to try now, with what he'd already done. Jeff got to his knees, took off his belt, and looped it about the horse's neck. He said in a commanding voice, "All right, let's go. Come on! Up! Up, boy! Up!" he pulled on the belt with all his strength with one hand and slapped with the other.

As if he understood, the horse lunged powerfully upward. One front leg pulled free and slammed on top of the mat of limbs. His body rose, then as his weight hit the mat, the leg broke through, dragging the brush down with the sinking leg. The mat hadn't been thick enough.

Jeff crept back to solid ground and began feverishly breaking off more brush and building a thicker mat. He had it almost thick enough to try when he heard the men returning. They were traveling slowly and talking. He grabbed the stallion's nose again.

Chad said, "Well, anyway, Pa, we got the mares back."

"Not hide nor hair of that stallion," Benny Wallace said, "That sure beats all."

"You suppose he just went off and left 'em?" Johnny Walsh asked.

"That don't make sense," Lem grumbled. "We should at least have spotted 'im."

"Maybe he's hightailed it outa the country for good," Benny said.

They had found the mares. Now Lem had no reason for shooting the stallion. They could help rescue the horse. Jeff was opening his mouth to shout when Lem's deadly voice said, "No tellin' what a stallion'll do. I'd rather of killed 'im. If he's gone, I'm bettin' he'll be back. Not a mare in the valley'll be safe as long as that red devil's around loose. I'll give a hundred dollars to the man that kills 'im."

Jeff held his breath while the little cavalcade passed on the other side of the brush. He waited until the sound of their traveling faded before releasing the horse's nose. He was alone now with the big red horse helplessly mired in the deadly muck.

Jeff could sense that the horse was beginning to get panicky again. Another futile struggle would only sink him deeper. He patted the big neck and began to talk. "Whoa, boy. Easy," he soothed. "You'll only make it worse. I'll make this mat of limbs thicker this time so you won't break though."

Jeff didn't know whether it was the sound of his voice or the touch of his hands that did it, but the horse became quiet again.

Jeff returned to gathering brush and piling it under the horse's chin. He got a great pile, spread it thick, and again worked it down along the legs as far as he could. Then he slapped him smartly on the neck and began to pull with all his strength. "Come on!" he shouted. "Up! Up! Now!"

The horse heaved himself upward. The same leg came out again. The muddy hoof slammed on top of the brush mat. It gave him leverage and his body began to rise above the water. His neck was stretched out straight. He groaned with effort. The freed front leg trembled with the strain upon it. "You're making it!" Jeff shouted. "You're making it! Come on! Come on!" Unmindful of the danger, Jeff lurched to his own feet and pulled with all his strength. The horse rose another inch.

Then the hoof broke through dragging brush under. He sank back into the muck again with a tired sigh. Jeff was so disappointed he began to cry.

The horse had sunk lower than before. The sluggish water was now creeping along his sides. Jeff dashed away the tears and began gathering more brush to start over again. He knew of nothing else to do. In time he built up a thick pile and tried again. He didn't do as well this time. The horse couldn't even get the one leg out. It seemed to Jeff he was too tired to try hard. Or maybe, he thought with sick fear, the horse was getting weaker or was giving up. He remembered reading somewhere that certain animals, when hopelessly trapped, just gave up and died. He wondered if horses did.

"Don't you quit on me," he begged. "You've got to keep trying."

Jeff knew he needed more than brush. Now the black muck was halfway up the horse's side. He quit gathering brush and looked for large limbs or poles that he could wedge under the animal's body to help hold him up. He scouted around for several hundred yards before he found four large ones. One at a time he dragged them out along the brush crawlway, and after digging in the muck with his hands and much shoving, he worked all four under the horse. Before he'd finished the sky darkened and it began to rain. He was already soaked and could get no wetter, but he began to shiver with cold. He had to go ashore several times to stand up and beat his arms and jump about to restore circulation.

The horse no longer struggled. He seemed to accept his fate. His head was not looking about, ears forward and alert. Now it sagged, resting on the matting Jeff had spread. Jeff knelt by the horse, petting and stroking him. There was nothing more he could do but wait for the slow suffocation when the black muck closed over the horse's head. "I should have called Lem and let him shoot you," he said thickly. "At least a bullet would have been quick and merciful."

- 5 -

THE BIG LIMBS Jeff had wedged under the horse's body helped, but not enough. He could not see the animal actually sinking into the sucking muck, but over a period of time he realized the horse had settled several inches lower.

The rain increased to a hard, pelting drive. Jeff began to shake. His teeth started to chatter. After a time the shaking passed and a sort of numbness came over him. Then he felt the muscles of the horse trembling. As big and strong as he was the cold was creeping into the stallion, too. Jeff patted and stroked his neck and murmured, "Just hold on. Hold on. That's what I'm doing. My dad'll come for me as soon as Hank gets to the store and tells him I wasn't in school today. He'll find us and get you out of here."

That was wishful thinking. Hank might not go to the store. Then his parents would think he'd stopped at home this time instead of going on to the store. His father wouldn't start looking until after they got home and found him gone. And even if Hank did tell them he hadn't been at school, they had no way of knowing where he'd taken off for. His father would have to start hunting blind. It might be hours before Fred Hunter came this way. By then it would be too late to save the stallion. Jeff dreaded the moment when the black muck would close over the horse's head.

He looked up at the weeping sky and tried to guess the time of day. But with no sun, he couldn't tell. He only knew he'd been here a long time. He thought of his lunch on the bank. There were two sandwiches, a piece of cake and an orange in the tin bucket. But he had no desire for food. He put both arms around the horse's neck and held his head up. He pressed his wet cold cheek against the velvety softness of the animal's nose and marveled dully that he'd never felt anything like it before. He didn't talk much because the animal was quiet now. Jeff just cradled the big head in his arms and stroked him. He felt that something went out of him to the stallion and they understood each other.

The day was waning. Dusk was creeping through the trees when Fred and Harve Sanders found them.

Fred crawled out on the mat and said gently, "All right, son. Let go of the horse and come back to shore."

"He'll drown if I let go," Jeff mumbled through blue lips.

"He'll drown if you don't," Fred said. "Harve and I will take over now and try to get him out. Come on, Jeff, let go and crawl back to solid ground."

"I thought you'd never come," Jeff managed. "I've been waiting and waiting."

"I'm here now. Come on."

"He's been stuck all day," Jeff rambled on. "I tried and tried to get him out."

"I know that. Now get out of here so we can work."

Jeff let go and the stallion's head dropped into the water, then was wearily raised again. Jeff crawled along the brush mat, but he was so cold and stiff Fred had to help him. Harve Sanders finally reached out and lifted him to his feet and held him while Fred slipped off his own coat and wrapped it about his son.

Harve Sanders was a short, stocky man, a trapper and hunter. He lived alone in a cabin a couple of miles back in the hills above the Hunters' place. The whole valley knew Harve and his little brown mare, Dolly, who followed him day after day like a dog while he hunted. She accepted any burden strapped to her back, whether it be a pack, deer, bear, or cougar. Now she stood a few feet off calmly looking at the trapped stallion.

Fred set Jeff down under a tree where it was fairly dry. "You stay put," he said, "Harve and I will see what we can do."

"How did you find me?"

"Hank came to the store and wanted to know if you were sick, said you weren't in school. Then I got it out of him where you'd gone Sunday and why. Then I figured what I'd do at your age. Why I'd come up here to try to drive the stallion out of the country so Lem couldn't kill him. You were mighty upset about it."

Jeff sat huddled under the thick branches of the tree and watched the two men try to rescue the horse. They cut more brush. Half of it they piled under the horse's chin as Jeff had done, the rest was stacked behind the stallion. Then Harve took a coil of rope from Dolly's saddle and Fred crawled out to the horse carrying one end. He carefully worked the rope under the horse's body, across his shoulders, then tied it. The other end was made fast to Dolly's saddle horn. Then both men went out on the mat. Fred was at the horse's head, Sanders behind.

Dolly stood at the edge of the solid ground calmly waiting as if she knew what was expected of her. "Now," Harve said, "when I tell Dolly to pull you haul on his head and I'll push and lift from behind. If he's got any fight left in him there's a chance to get him out. All right, ready? Dolly," he shouted, "take it away!"

There in the driving rain with one man pulling on the horse's head, one pushing and lifting behind, and Dolly digging in with all her nine hundred pounds, they fought to save the big stallion.

Fred Hunter yanked on the strap around the neck and yelled to rouse the sluggish animal. Sanders cut him hard across his hindquarters with a switch and added his voice to Fred's. Dolly's driving feet slipped. She almost fell, caught herself, and lunged into the line. The mired horse surged forward convulsively and began to fight. But the black muck had a death grip that had been holding for hours. Nothing happened.

Jeff's heart sank. The horse was doomed. He had felt it all along.

Then Fred let out a yell and Sanders shouted, "Now!" and struck the horse smartly across the rump. "Now! Now!"

Jeff found himself standing, hardly believing his eyes. The horse's back was slowly rising inch by agonizing inch above the sucking muck. As though he knew he was coming free the stallion began struggling frantically. One front foot came out, then the other. Somewhere he found a bit of solid footing and lunged upward with one tremendous effort. Jeff wanted to cheer. The horse was almost out of the bog when he slipped and fell. Gallant little Dolly dragged him the remaining feet to solid earth. He scrambled weakly to his feet and stood, head down, the heavy muscles of his legs trembling with exhaustion. The driving rain began to wash the mud from his heaving sides.

Jeff ran to him and put his arms around his neck, "You made it! You made it! I knew you would."

"All right," Fred said, "now you get for home. You're soaking wet. You'll be lucky if you don't catch pneumonia."

"Ride Dolly," Sanders said. "She'll take you home faster." With one sweep of powerful arms he lifted Jeff and set him astride Dolly.

"You'll bring the stallion?"

"We'll bring him," Fred promised. "Now get going."

Jeff gathered up the reins, turned Dolly, and headed for home. He bent his head against the lash of the rain. He was so cold he clung to the saddle horn with both hands for fear of falling.

Lilian met him at the head of the lane and led Dolly to the kitchen door. When he slipped out of the saddle he'd have fallen had she not grabbed his arm. "Hurry upstairs and take off those wet clothes and rub yourself dry with one of the big, rough towels. Rub hard to get the circulation going again. Then put on dry clothes."

"All right," he said. "What about Dolly?"

"I'll take care of Dolly and be right in."

It didn't take long to strip off his wet clothing and towel himself dry. He felt warmer but he was still shivering. The cold seemed to have gone right to his bones.

When he came downstairs Lilian shoved a cup of steaming milk in front of him. "Get that inside you. It'll help drive off the chill."

He was so cold he had to use both hands to hold the cup, and the first gulp seemed to burn a hot trail all the way to his stomach. But it tasted wonderful and pleasant warmth began to spread through him. He finished the milk and Lilian refilled it. He finished the second cup and said, "I'm fine now." Suddenly he was ravenously hungry.

Lilian had a steaming plate of food before him in a minute. Then she sat across the table and said, "Now. Maybe you'd like to fill me in on where you've been and what you've been doing all this day you were supposed to be in school. You've had me worried to death. I was imagining all sorts of things."

"I'm sorry," he said.

"Start talking. I want to hear everything from the minute you walked out that door this morning heading for school until you came back through it looking like a drowned rat. The complete story."

"You mean everything?"

"Every last word and thought." She laid her hands flat on the table.

He told her everything, ending with, "I left my lunch pail and books up there. The rain ruined the books. I'm sorry."

"So they got the stallion out and turned him loose. Good. I didn't like the idea of such a beautiful animal being killed."

"But mom, they're bringing him here now. They sent me on ahead on Dolly because I was so wet."

"Bringing him here!" Lilian shook her head. "Well, I never! I just never. You and your father are like two peas in a pod."

"What's that mean?"

"What you did today is exactly the kind of crazy stunt he'd have pulled at your age. I know, I lived on the opposite end of the block from him." She smiled, "Maybe that was what I liked about him to begin with. And it's part of what I like about you. But why bring the horse here?"

"We've got a barn and plenty of room," Jeff pointed out.

"They could turn him loose like he was before."

"If they did, Lem would be after him again. And he's cold and wet and hungry and tired. Besides," Jeff added as a clincher, "I found him."

Lilian nodded soberly, "I knew that one was coming."

There was the sound of voices and Jeff and Lilian hurried to the door. Fred and Harve were coming down the lane. The big red horse walked between them, head down, the picture of exhaustion. The rain, which was beginning to slack off, had washed off much of the mud clinging to his sides. But it was still obvious he'd spent the day in a mud hole.

"You poor thing," Lilian said. "You look beat."

"He is beat," Fred said. "Get a bucket of warm water and some rags to wash him off. I'll be back for it in a minute."

Lilian called after them, "Harve, I didn't unsaddle Dolly. I didn't know how. I put her in a stall and gave her hay and grain."

"Thanks," Harve answered.

When Fred came into the kitchen for the rags and warm water Jeff grabbed a coat to go with him.

"Leave that coat alone, young man," Lilian said. "You came home shaking like a straw in the wind and looking like you'd crawled out of the river. You want to chase out again? No."

"I'm warm now. I feel fine. I've got to see him."

"Why?" Lilian demanded.

"I found him, Mom."

"So you told me."

Fred was studying his son. "You feel all right? Not cold or too tired or anything. No chill?"

"I feel fine," Jeff insisted. "Honest."

"He'd say that if he was dying, just so he got to go out to see that horse," Lilian said.

"Nothing like being a kid," Fred smiled. "Bounce right back. Might as well let him come. He looks all right. And the barn's warm."

"Well," Lilian considered, "all right. But if you get a cold over this, or if you even sniffle once, I'll fill you so full of castor oil you'll wish you'd never seen that barn or horse. Still want to go?"

"Yes."

"Then I'm coming, too."

It was warm inside the barn. The lit lantern was hanging from a nail. In the yellow shine Jeff saw Trixie in her stanchion and Dolly in one of the two stalls. The stallion was in the box-stall. With a gunny sack Harve was rubbing off the worst of the remaining mud. Both men began to wash the horse. Then they dried him with more sacks. He stood quietly accepting the ministrations. Harve put hay on the floor in front of him and he started to eat while they worked on him. His red coat began to glow in the lantern light.

"This horse is used to people," Harve observed. "He accepts our workin' around him like he expected it. Like it was his due."

"Where do you suppose he came from?" Fred asked.

"I couldn't begin to guess."

Jeff and Lilian stood in the open box-stall door and Lilian said, "Why, he's beginning to look almost beautiful."

"A little thin," Harve said. "But a good feed of oats everyday will soon bring his weight up again."

Jeff couldn't take his eyes off the horse. "Is he going to be all right, Harve?" he asked.

"Going to be? He's all right now." He grinned at Jeff, "He's healthy as a horse."

At the sound of Jeff's voice the stallion turned his head and found the boy. His ears came forward and his head came up. He nickered softly. Jeff walked in and the horse thrust out his head, nibbled at Jeff's shirt, and nickered again.

"Will you look at that?" Harve said. "Jeff's got a friend."

"I was with him all day." Jeff patted the big head.

"Could be the reason," Harve agreed. "Then again, maybe he associates you with somebody he liked."

"How do you mean?" Lilian asked.

"I'm not sure. But remember he's not a wild horse. Maybe Jeff talks or looks like somebody he trusted, someone who fed and cared for 'im. Maybe being with him all day, trying to help him is part of it, too. Animals have their likes and dislikes the same as we do. He tolerates Fred and me, accepts what we do for him like he expects it. But the minute Jeff shows up he begins talkin' to him and nibblin' at his shirt. Jeff's the one."

Harve stood back, hands on hips, and studied the big horse who was pushing at Jeff with his head. "Something mighty odd about you," he observed. "You're used to being handled. You walk in here calm as you please, a place you've never seen before, take this box-stall as if you knew it was yours. Sure wish you could talk. I'll bet what you could say would be real interesting." He glanced at Fred, "Now you got him, what're you gonna do with him?"

Jeff held his breath waiting his father's answer. When Fred just stood there and frowned Jeff said in a low, careful voice, "Keep him."

"Keep him!" Lilian said. "What do we need a horse for?"

"Everybody in the country needs a horse," Fred said.

"I found him," Jeff pointed out, "and he doesn't belong to anybody around here. It's loser's weepers, finder's keepers. Isn't it, Harve?"

Harve had got the curry comb and brush and was working on the horse's tangled mane. "That's how we used to say."

"You know better than that, Jeff," Lilian said sharply.

"Trouble is," Fred said, "he is an owned horse. Harve, you got any ideas on that?"

Sanders kept working on the mane and said thoughtfully, "One time or another I've seen most of the horses in this upper valley, I guess. I'd remember the likes of this one. He's not the kind people cotton to around here. He's not built to pull a plow or wagon and he's no cayuse. He could be from a long ways off and wandered down into our valley followin' his nose. Animal like this can travel fast and far. This long-haired coat he's wearing says he's been in the high country where it's cold. He had to be there some time for it to grow out. He hasn't had a curry comb and brush on him in months. I'd guess he's from east of the mountains or even out of state. No doubt somebody's looked for him. But after being lost as long as he appears to have been, and traveling as many miles from his home range as he likely has, the odds on finding him are practically zero. The chances of locating his former owner are just as slim. Whoever lost this horse probably quit looking long ago."

"Then we've got three choices as I see it," Fred said. "Keep him, try to find his owner, or turn him loose."

"You can't travel all over the state knocking on doors and asking if someone lost a horse," Lilian said.

"Exactly."

"If you turn him loose, Lem'll shoot him," Jeff said quickly.

"That he will," Harve agreed. "This fellow will start right out to gather himself another string of mares. Next thing Lem and the whole valley will be up in arms."

"Then we've only one choice."

"We don't need a horse," Lilian insisted.

"We're not farmers if that's what you mean. But we can use a horse. Jeff could ride it to school. You'd like that, wouldn't you?" Fred grinned at his son.

"Yes! Oh, yes!" Jeff almost choked on his enthusiasm. He stroked the horse as if he already had him.

"And summer's coming. There'll be picnics, ball games to go to, Sunday drives we could take."

"We don't have a buggy."

"There's that new one in the shed back of the store. We might as well use it. Nobody's even asked about buying it."

Lilian was not yet ready to accept keeping the horse. "We don't have a saddle for Jeff. And maybe this horse can't be ridden or hitched to a buggy. And you're not a horse trainer, Fred," she added as a clincher.

"Well." Fred scratched his head and grinned at Harve.

Harve, who'd been currying and watching Jeff, said

quietly, "I've got an old saddle Jeff can have. That is if you decide to keep him. As for ridin'him; I got a theory about this horse. I'd just like to try a little experiment if you don't mind. Come here, Jeff."

With a sweep he lifted Jeff and set him astride the stallion's back. The horse turned his head curiously, looked at Jeff, then returned to eating. "What I figured," Harve smiled. "Maybe nobody else can ride this animal, but I'll bet Jeff can do near about anything with him. As for the buggy, you'd just have to try and see. You can get down now, Jeff."

Jeff slid off and stood looking at his mother, holding his breath, waiting her next objection.

"He looks awfully big for a boy to handle," Lilian said doubtfully. "Suppose, just suppose he's mean?"

"You saw him just now," Harve said. "Size has nothing to do with meanness."

Lilian kept looking at the horse, frowning, thoughtful. Finally she spread her hands, "I'm fresh out of arguments."

"Then he's ours! He's ours!" Jeff began dancing about the horse. He threw his arms around the big neck and cried, "You're ours. You hear that? Ours!"

His father's sober voice brought him up short. "It's not that simple. He still belongs to somebody. We've got to make some sort of effort to find the legal owner. Best thing I know of is to run an ad describing the horse in the Springfield paper for a couple of weeks."

"If nobody comes to claim him, then he's ours?" Jeff asked breathlessly.

Fred shook his head. "He'll never be really ours. Any time somebody can prove legal ownership they can claim him. So you've got to be prepared to give him up if that time ever comes, whether it's a year or five years from now. Do you understand that?"

"Maybe nobody will ever come for him," Jeff said hopefully. "Harve says he's been lost a long time."

"Even so," Fred said, "the possibility's there. You got that straight?"

"Yes. Do I have to wait until the ad quits running in the paper before I can ride him?"

"No, I guess not."

Harve put the curry comb and brush on the shelf. He got Dolly and prepared to leave. "I'll bring the saddle down tomorrow about the time you get home from school."

"Harve," Lilian asked, "what kind of horse is he?"

"You mean bloodlines and such? I don't know. Been around horses most of my life. The kind we've got in the valley, and cayuses. But this fellow doesn't fit into anything I've ever seen around here. One thing I know. He's a fighter, and that's bred into an animal. A lot of horses I know would have given up after spending all day in the bog like he did. But not this feller. When it came time to fight, he reared up and gave it as big a try as you'll ever see."

"Is he all right to leave alone tonight?" Jeff asked.

"He's fine. He's had a good bit of hay. And before you came out I gave him a little of the cow's grain. But leave him in this box-stall until I get here. If you let him out in the pasture he'll jump the fence sure as shootin' and be off again. We've got to add another board to the fence to make it higher."

"We can't expect you to spend your time down here," Fred said.

"I'm through trappin' for the year. Spring's almost here. But I'll send Jeff a man-sized bill one of these days," Harve said and left.

Jeff wanted to stay with the horse, but Lilian said, "Nothing doing. You're going to bed right now and get a good night's sleep. You've had a big day."

"But, Mom, I feel fine. It's warm in here. And he'll get lonesome alone in a strange place."

"He doesn't look lonesome to me. And Harve said he walked in as if he knew he belonged. You come on. And no more arguments."

"But I'm not sleepy."

"You will be."

Fred laughed, "You're wound up tight as a spring about

to bust. Come on, son. The horse will be here in the morning."

Back in the house, as Jeff started to climb the stairs, Fred reminded him, "Don't start building your hopes on that horse. The ad I'm going to run in the paper will be seen by quite a few thousand people. Somebody could claim him within the next few days."

"I know," Jeff said.

"I put a couple of hot rocks in your bed," Lilian said. "You leave them there."

"I will." He went up the stairs and got ready for bed. The rocks were two lumps down where his feet would be. The last thing before climbing into bed he looked out the window at the barn.

He thought of the first glimpse he'd had of the stallion from this window in a driving rain. And now the horse was safe right out there in the barn. A terrible impatience grew and grew inside him. He didn't see how he could wait for tomorrow. The rain had stopped. The clouds were thinning out. The moon was about to break through. A single star shone brightly over the barn roof. He remembered the rhyme his mother had smilingly given him one night when they first moved here and he'd discovered that the stars out in the country seemed much brighter than in the city. Of course, Jeff knew it didn't mean a thing. But just in case, he repeated it to himself:

> Star light, star bright,
> First star I've seen tonight
> I wish I would, I wish I might,
> Have the wish I wish tonight.

He got into bed and shoved his feet down against the warm rocks. That star shining over the barn was a wonderful omen for good.

- 6 -

HANK AND JEFF pounded down the dirt road side by side, arms pumping, books and lunch buckets swinging wildly. They turned into Hunters' lane, dashed past the house, and out to the barn. Dolly was in a stall munching hay. An old scarred saddle hung over one wall of the stall. Harve was in the box-stall with the big red stallion currying and brushing him.

At sight of Jeff the horse nickered, his ears came forward, and he stretched his neck and nibbled experimentally at Jeff's jacket. Jeff patted him between the eyes and said triumphantly to Hank, "I told you I had him."

"Yup," Hank agreed, "you sure enough got 'im all right." Then he just stood there looking at the horse. "He looks bigger'n he did last Sunday."

"That's because he's in a box-stall and not standing in the middle of Buttercup Canyon."

"I guess so."

Jeff looked at Harve, "He's all right, isn't he?"

"He's fine. Just fine."

"Can you tell any more about him?"

"You mean like where he came from or who owned him? That kind of thing?"

"Yes."

"No more'n I told you last night. He's used to being handled by people and he's surprisingly gentle. There's no way of knowin' any more."

"You think you can ride 'im?" Hank asked. "When you gonna ride 'im?"

Jeff looked at Harve.

"Now's as good time as any to try. I brought the saddle. It doesn't look like much, but it's usable."

"You think I can ride him?"

"I don't know. Maybe."

"I sat on his back last night."

"That was different. You didn't have a saddle on him then and he was completely tuckered out."

"He might buck me off?"

"Today's another day. He's rested. Anyhow you'll never know until you try."

The boys watched while Harve put the saddle on, cinched it, adjusted the stirrups, and led the horse outside. "All right, come on. Climb up on the water trough. I'll hold him while you get in the saddle."

Jeff's mouth was dry. His heart was hammering.

Harve brought the horse close and held his head while Jeff settled himself in the saddle. "Now," Harve said, "grip with your knees and thighs and push down in the stirrups. That's it. Now walk him around the corral. Just walk."

Jeff swallowed nervously. It was a long way to the ground if he was bucked off. He clucked and shook the reins. The horse stepped out calmly, quietly, and walked around the corral following the fence line. They circled the corral for about ten minutes and Harve said, "Just like an old farm plug."

"Can I take him out in the pasture?" Jeff asked.

"Wait until we add another board on the fence for height. He could sail right over that if he has a mind to. I'd say this's pretty good for the first day."

Jeff rode up to the water trough and got off. The big horse nickered, and blew his breath in the boy's face, and nibbled delicately at his shirt. Jeff patted his neck, his eyes shining. "I can ride him, Harve. I can ride him."

"You can for a fact," Harve agreed. "Like I said, he takes

to you."

"How about me riding"im?" Hank asked.

"You might," Harve said. "But I've got a feeling that just anybody can't ride this fellow."

"Jeff did. I can. He's just a horse. How'll he know it ain't Jeff?"

"He'll know all right. But come on." Harve held the horse while Hank climbed on the water trough and into the saddle. Hank picked up the reins and Harve stepped back. "Come on," Hank said impatiently, "Giddap." He kicked the horse in the ribs with his heels. "Get movin'."

The big horse looked around. His ears went back tight to his head. The next instant his head was down and his back humped. Hank was shooting into the air when Harve's big hands jerked him off. The horse immediately became quiet again.

"What's th' matter with 'im?" Hank yelled angrily. "I didn't do nothin' that'd hurt 'im."

"You weren't Jeff in that saddle," Harve said. "I don't think anybody else is going to ride this horse."

"Why?"

"Horses are like people. Some they like, some they don't."

"That's crazy."

"Maybe. But don't try to ride him again. You could get bad hurt."

"Well, I'm goin'home," Hank grumbled. "I don't want nothin' to do with a crazy horse. He needs a good larrupin', that's what." He went off up the lane.

"You might as well ride around a few more minutes while I get a hammer and nails," Harve said to Jeff. "Then you and I will make this fence a little higher. There's a whole pile of boards back of the barn we can use."

So Jeff walked the big stallion around and around the corral, and the horse only turned his sharp ears back now and then to catch the boy's words as he talked to him.

When Harve was ready they removed the saddle and put

him back into the box-stall. Then they went to work on the pasture fence. Jeff dragged the boards to Harve and helped hold them while the trapper nailed them to the posts.

They worked until Lilian came home from the store. She tried to talk Harve into staying for supper, but he refused.

"Got grub at home I got to eat or it'll spoil. See you in the morning. And, Jeff, don't let that horse out in the pasture until we finish making the fence higher."

Harve and Jeff spent all the next day, Saturday, working on the fence. The added board made it almost six feet high. Trixie was in the pasture but she paid no attention to them. Harve let the horse into the corral where he trotted back and forth. He stuck his nose over the high fence and nickered at Jeff every time he passed near carrying another board for Harve. Finally, when they were about three-quarters finished Harve said, "Might as well let him into the pasture now. I've a hunch he'll stay. If he tries to jump this lower part, he'll have to come near me, and I can scare him away."

When Jeff opened the corral gate the horse charged into the pasture, mane and tail flying, kicking up his heels and shaking his head. He thundered across the pasture and Jeff held his breath as he neared the high section without slackening speed. The last second he turned and raced along fence. Harve watched, hammer in hand.

Jeff finally yelled, "Hey, come here. Come on." At the sound of the boy's voice the horse turned and charged straight at him. Fear welled up in Jeff. He was about to turn and run into the corral and slam the gate when the horse braced to a stop, then walked quietly up to him, nibbled at his shirt, and blew his breath in the boy's face. Jeff patted him and said, "I like you, too. Come on." Thereafter, he tagged Jeff back and forth across the pasture and galloped circles around him while Jeff carried boards to Harve. Finally he tired of that and went to make friends with Trixie.

Harve said, "Let's take five." They sat with their backs against the fence to rest. Harve studied the horse nibbling grass near Trixie and asked, "You thought of a name for him?"

Jeff had spent a lot of time at school writing down all the names he could think of. He took the paper from his pocket and read them to Harve, "Red, Big Boy, Lightning, because he was so fast. Thunder, Storm, both because of the night I first saw him. Flash, Jim, Buttons. . . ." He had about twenty names. Harve tore a sliver from a board, sat picking his teeth, and listened.

"You like any of those?" Jeff asked.

"Not especially. Oughta be somethin' special. Lotta horses in this valley named Bill, Flash and Buttons and John."

"How do you mean special?"

"Well, he's a pretty special horse, ain't he?"

"He's the most special horse in this valley. Maybe in the whole world."

"You're takin' in a lotta territory. But he's special in this valley and to you anyway. Then he needs a name that's different from all these others. One that means just him and that fits."

"How do you mean?"

"Maybe somethin' like how you found him, or what he's like," Harve said vaguely. "Like Quicksand, cause he got stuck in some, or Midnight, cause you first seen him at midnight, didn't you? Somethin' like that."

Jeff thought of the first night he'd seen the horse. Dark, windy, driving rain, blinding lightning, crashing thunder that shook the house. Something unreal, ghostly, had pricked at his scalp as the horse tore up the lane, mane and tail flying, eyes wild, seeming a part of the storm itself. He'd seen a picture of a ghost story of just such a night with scary creatures. Those creatures had fit the picture and the story. The horse had fit the night of that storm. He said the word aloud. "Goblin!"

Harve looked at him. "Now there's a name like no other horse in the valley's ever had. I like it. That's a dandy. It fits him. Running around stealin' mares at night, getting caught in that bog hole, outrunnin' Lem's Blackie, like he was standin' still, Benny said. And we don't know a thing about him. Everything about him is sort of unreal and spooky. Yes, sir, I'd say that's a real appropriate name for him. You like it?"

Jeff said the name several times. He rolled the syllables on his tongue and liked the sound. "Goblin," he said. "Goblin." He stood up and yelled, "Goblin! Goblin, come here, boy."

The horse left off his eating and trotted over shaking his head and snorting delicately. Jeff patted his neck and rubbed his nose and smiled at Harve, "He knows his name already."

"I wouldn't be surprised." Harve rose and picked up the hammer. "You oughta carry a few sugar cubes in your pocket. When you call him and he comes, give him one and pretty soon he'll always come."

"I will." Jeff patted Goblin. "Harve, do you think anybody will see that notice Dad put in the paper about finding Goblin?"

"That Springfield paper gets to most all this upper valley. A lotta people will see it. I don't think Goblin's from the valley. But somebody might know where he belongs. There's no way of tellin' what might happen with that notice. None at all. If I was you, I wouldn't bank too much on keepin' him. Just enjoy him whether it's a day, two days, two weeks, or two years."

"I hope nobody comes for him."

"Loser's weepers?"

"Yes."

"Then we'd better finish this fence."

Fred brought home the Springfield paper with the notice in it. Jeff read it and hated it for its size, its accurate description of Goblin, where he'd been found, and where he was now. The most damning line of all, that he wished he could erase, was at the bottom: Anyone who can prove ownership can have the horse any time. He wanted to ask his father if it had been necessary to add that. But he didn't.

His mother seldom called him in the morning now. He got up, dressed, and crept quietly down the stairs before either of his parents was awake. He'd stop in the kitchen, take a couple of sugar cubes, and go down to the barn to see Goblin.

The grass was usually heavy with dew. He watched for tracks where rabbits or a pheasant had passed. Maybe a mouse had knocked the drops off the grass blades. The air was sharp and clean. Some mornings there was a dusting of frost on the roofs of the house and barn. The stars were still out and the moon would be plunging toward the rim of the mountains. Often in the chill silence he heard a rooster's first announcement. Birds would be making sleepy noises in the nearby brush. The day would be just coming into being way off at the edge of the night.

The barn smelled warm and close. Trixie was usually lying down chewing her cud. Goblin was always looking for him, his head over the top of the box-stall. He'd nicker a greeting, his sharp ears forward and paw at the bottom boards with his front feet. Jeff would give him a sugar cube, and his feeding of oats and hay. He'd brush and curry Goblin's coat, talking all the while. Then he'd lead the horse out into the corral for his morning drink and watch him bury his nose in the cold water right up to the nostrils. If it weren't raining he'd slip the halter and let Goblin into the pasture and watch him race around the fence and kick up his heels. Goblin could stay out until Fred came from the house to milk Trixie. Then Jeff put the horse back in the box-stall, fed him the remaining sugar cube, and fussed over him until Fred finished milking.

Jeff no longer stopped to admire the black pony, though he came to the fence and nickered a welcome. The apple he'd saved from lunch was now for Goblin.

Hank complained that he was always in too much of a rush. "For gosh sakes, what's the hurry? That old horse'll be there. You'd think he'd run away or somebody's stole him, the way you rush off."

Jeff liked to torture himself during the day with the thought that maybe Goblin would be gone when he returned from school. Maybe someone had seen the ad and come for him. He was always frightened and apprehensive when he finally ran down the lane, and relieved when he swung the barn door open and Goblin's head appeared above the top of the box-stall as he nickered his welcome. He'd feed the stallion the apple and pet him and croon, "I sure am glad to see you." Goblin would contentedly crunch the apple then blow his breath in the boy's face and nibble at his shirt and toss his head as if he understood. With the passing of each day a little of the tension inside Jeff let go.

Some nights Hank came with him and watched as he saddled Goblin, standing on a box to put the saddle on. Then he'd lead him outside for his drink. Afterward Jeff would climb to the top of the trough and into the saddle. Hank plainly wanted to ask to ride again, but he never did. When Jeff took Goblin into the pasture Hank would leave and head for the blacksmith shop.

Jeff would ride around and around the pasture until Lilian came from the store.

Harve stopped by one day. Jeff galloped Goblin back and forth across the pasture while Harve looked on. "You're doing fine. The more you're with him, the more he'll get to understand what you want till you won't hardly have to use the reins."

While his father milked, Jeff wanted to spend his time with Goblin, but Fred insisted that he punch the straw sack and keep up on his practice. Jeff always managed to squeeze in a few minutes with Goblin before they left the barn.

No one came to claim Goblin. Jeff could barely restrain himself from bragging about the horse at school. Several times Hank said something but no one paid any attention and Jeff gave him warning looks.

Billy Decker brought the newspaper ad to school. At noon while all the kids sat on the porch steps eating lunch he read it aloud. "Your old man's trying to make out like he got that big red stallion that's been running loose," he scoffed. "Me and Pa and Chad and Benny and Johnny Walsh chased him all one day and couldn't catch him. I suppose your old man run him down on foot, huh?" he said to Jeff. When Jeff didn't answer. "If you got him, how come you don't ride him to school, clodhopper? How come you're still walkin'?"

"He's got 'im," Hank burst out angrily. "Jeff rides 'im every night in the pasture. Go down and see."

"I'll bet it's some old crow bait they found someplace, and old man Hunter's just trying to act big." The kids grinned. A couple of the girls giggled.

"Have you sure enough got that stallion?" Bob Lyons asked.

Jeff wanted to say he did and invite them all to come see Goblin. But suppose when he got home tonight someone had come to claim him and he was already gone. He could never prove it then. Or maybe somebody would come to claim him tomorrow or the next day and his victory tonight would be hollow. So he walked into the schoolhouse without answering.

Mr. Jacoby was standing by the window, hands stuffed in his pockets, scowling. He said to Jeff, "I saw the notice in the paper, Jeff. Of course you do have the horse?"

"Yes, sir." Jeff told Mr. Jacoby how he'd found Goblin and why he didn't ride him to school and couldn't answer Bob Lyons' question.

"I think your parents were right that you don't ride him to school until that notice is withdrawn from the paper. The owner could show up any time. So his name's Goblin. Very appropriate. Don't let Billy's riding you get under your skin. He's a little jealous because *they* didn't catch the horse. Think how foolish he's going to feel the day you come riding to school on Goblin."

Hank came in muttering darkly, "Just wait. Someday! Someday!"

"Someday what, Henry?" Mr. Jacoby asked.

Hank looked up, then grumbled, "Just someday, that's all."

On the fourteenth day Jeff thought school would never let out. Again he tortured himself with the thought that maybe on this last day someone had come for Goblin. He might not be in his box-stall at home. Maybe whoever had come for him hadn't seen the notice before, or had to come a long way. The door to the stall would yawn open, the stall empty. When Mr.

Jacoby finally dismissed school, Jeff tore out the door and down the road not waiting for Hank who was still fooling around his desk.

He raced breathlessly down the lane into the barn. The first thing he saw was Goblin's head over the top of the stall. His sharp ears were forward and he nickered a welcome.

That night when Fred came home from the store he was carrying a package. Jeff had exercised Goblin for a time in the pasture but returned him to the box-stall early so he could talk to his father. He dashed up the lane into the kitchen where Fred was taking off his coat. The package lay on the table.

"Dad, this is the fourteenth day. You said you'd run the notice two weeks and then if nobody came Goblin was mine. Remember? Then he's mine now, isn't he? He's mine?"

"I guess maybe he is," Fred smiled. "I didn't really expect anyone to answer that notice and claim him, after all the time he seems to have been lost and the distance he must have traveled. I did it just to be as sure as I could. As for Goblin being legally yours, that can't be until you've got a bill of sale. You understand that."

"Yes, sir. But if nobody ever comes for him. . . ."

"Why then we just keep him."

"Then he's mine."

"For all practical purposes I'd say that's right."

"I can ride him to school tomorrow?"

"I don't know about that," Lilian said doubtfully. "Goblin's a lot of horse for a boy."

"I've been riding him in the pasture for two weeks," Jeff pointed out. "He hasn't thrown me once. He hasn't even tried."

"He'll be all right," Fred said. "Harve said from the first that Goblin took to Jeff for some odd reason. That seems to be correct. I've watched them. I see no reason he can't ride to school."

"Well, all right. But you be careful," Lilian warned. "I don't want to hear of you trying anything fancy or clever."

"What kind of fancy or clever?" Jeff asked.

"I haven't the faintest idea. Just don't try it."

"I won't," Jeff promised.

Fred handed him the package, "Go ahead, unwrap it."

"Mine?" Jeff asked.

"Sure."

Jeff unwrapped the package and found a new pair of chocolate brown cowboy boots with pointed toes, high heels, and scrollwork along the sides. There was also a belt with a huge silver buckle with a bucking horse etched in the metal.

"Figured these would go well with Goblin and the saddle," Fred said.

Jeff looked at them and felt them, "Gee!" he said. "Well, gee!"

"Try the boots on," Fred said. "They should be your size."

Jeff kicked off his clodhoppers and slid his feet into the boots. They fit, but his feet looked a little odd with the pointed toes. The big belt buckle, bigger even than Billy Decker's, cut into his stomach a little when he bent over. But he didn't care. He walked around the room feeling a little odd because the high heels threw him forward.

He smiled self-consciously at Fred and Lilian. "Guess I won't be wearing those old clodhoppers much any more. Gee! Thanks. The belt's swell, too. And the buckle. Gee!" He kept walking around the room.

Suddenly he bolted out the door and raced down the lane. He had to show Goblin.

- 7 -

JEFF WAS UP extra early. He had Goblin fed, watered, curried, and brushed long before Fred came out to milk. He was so excited he could hardly eat breakfast.

Lilian reminded him, "Young man, you don't leave this table until you've finished your cereal and eaten at least one slice of toast."

Fred helped him saddle Goblin and boosted him into the saddle. He hung a halter on the saddle horn and warned, "Leave him in the stall in the barn. Don't leave him out in the pasture with the other horses. That fence at school is pretty low for the likes of Goblin. Be sure the halter's well tied to the manger, give him a little hay in the morning, and be sure to water him at noon."

Lilian handed him his books and lunch pail and patted Goblin's neck. "Don't you get rambunctious and buck Jeff off," she warned. They stood side by side and watched Jeff ride up the lane and turn into the road. He looked back and waved before he rode out of sight.

Jeff was late this time so Hank was sitting on the big rock waiting. Hank stood up and brushed off his pants, "I figured you'd probably ride 'im today. How 'bout me gettin' up behind you? He can carry two easy."

"He'd buck. You know how he did that time you tried to ride him." He didn't want Hank riding behind even if Goblin would let him. This was his horse. He'd been dreaming of this morning a long time. It would be the first time the kids would see him on Goblin. Jeff wanted all the glory for himself.

Hank trudged along in the opposite wagon track. The black colt came down to the corner of the Decker land, hung his head over the rail fence, and nickered. Jeff paid no attention to him.

Hank said, "Got new boots, too, cowboy boots."

"And a belt." Jeff twisted so Hank could see the big silver buckle.

Hank scowled and kicked his coppertoed clodhoppers against the dirt wall of the wagon track. "You sure are all duded up. Maybe I'll get me a horse."

"Thought you didn't like 'em."

"It beats walkin'. Get me a big red bandana and a hat, too. Maybe I'll even get a pair of spurs, with rolls big as silver dollars, that jingle when you walk. Yes, sir, maybe I just will."

Goblin paced along lifting his feet high, neck arched, sharp ears working back and forth as he looked about interestedly. He kept snorting softly and pretending he wanted to break into a headlong gallop, but Jeff held a tight rein and spoke to him every few seconds.

The kids were outside playing "anty-over the schoolhouse" when they arrived. The game stopped and they gathered around. Jeff pulled up Goblin. He sat there and let them look. The picture of Jeff and the big stallion was mirrored in every kid's eyes. Jeff's heart was in his throat with pride. He didn't trust his voice.

Hank said proudly, sharing some of Jeff's glory because they were friends, "He's got new boots, and look at that silver buckle, a buckin' horse on it. Show 'em the buckle, Jeff."

Jeff twisted so they could all see the buckle.

Before the shiny boots, the silver buckle, and the magnificent horse they were speechless.

Billy Decker came from the barn and said, "Just a show-off horse, like in a circus. He ain't no good for nothin'. Bet he couldn't drive a thirsty cow to water. And that old saddle horn wouldn't hold a rabbit if you roped him."

"Maybe not," Hank piped up, "but he run Blackie right

off his legs."

"Didn't no such thing. We couldn't get close to him, that's all. Blackie was carryin' Pa, and he weighs two hundred pounds. This horse wasn't carryin' nothin'."

"What's his name?" one of the girls asked.

"Goblin," Jeff said. "His name's Goblin."

"That's a crazy name for a horse," Billy said. "Why don'tcha call him Red or somethin' like that? Give him a name that means something."

"I think it's a good name," Bob Lyons said. "I like it. I'll bet he can run. He looks fast. You say he outrun Lem's Blackie?"

"Benny Wallace and Johnny Walsh said he did," Jeff said.

"And there was five of them and they couldn't catch him," Hank added.

"I'd like to see him run," Bob said. "Billy's Snow Flake is the fastest horse here at school. How about you and him having a race at noon hour?"

"A race!" the kids began jumping up and down. "Good! A race! A race!"

"Well, how about it?" Bob asked.

"All right," Jeff agreed.

Billy scowled. The kids kept yelling. "A race! A race!"

"All right," Billy agreed. "I'll show you this noon that he just looks good. He really ain't."

Jeff thought about the race all morning. He hoped Goblin wouldn't disgrace them both. Harve had said you never could tell what a horse would do when pitted against another. Sometimes they refused to run, or bucked or something.

The whole school was on the porch to see the race. They sat on the steps, opened their lunch pails, and were eating while Jeff and Billy went to saddle their horses. Even Mr. Jacoby watched, leaning against the door frame, eating a sandwich.

Billy was ready first. Jeff was cinching up his saddle when Billy came into the stall and said, "Listen, clodhopper, you try to beat me and I'll give you another lickin'. I'll black both your eyes till you can't see and bloody your nose plenty. You just remember that." Then he led Snow Flake out.

A minute later Jeff followed.

Hank was the starter. He'd drawn a line through the dirt for a starting point. They'd race to the turn in the road, about a quarter mile, turn and come back. They'd start when Hank dropped his handkerchief and yelled, "Go!"

Snow Flake seemed to know what was expected. He'd been in a number of these races. Jeff had trouble just getting Goblin to the starting line and holding him there. Goblin stamped his feet, chewed on the bit, and looked about, sharp ears jumping back and forth.

At Hank's yelled, "Go!" and the dropping of the hand-kerchief Snow Flake was off. She had a hundred foot lead before Goblin got the idea. Then he leaped forward with a speed that threw Jeff backward in the saddle. The firm grip he had on the reins, the wild grab he made for the horn were all that kept him from being blown off.

He had galloped Goblin across the pasture, but that speed was nothing compared to this. His head stretched out. He seemed to lunge at the distance separating him from Snow Flake. The rush of wind almost snatched Jeff's breath away. The dirt road was a blur beneath his driving legs. Never had Jeff felt such a tremendous surge of power. Before him Snow Flake was straining ahead, but he appeared to be coming backward at a surprising rate. Jeff passed him several hundred yards short of the bend.

Jeff tried to stop Goblin, to turn him, but the horse wanted to keep running straight ahead. He was a good fifty yards past the turn before Jeff remembered to haul his head around hard with one rein. When he finally got Goblin turned and lined out Billy was on his way back with a greater lead than ever. Goblin took out after him as if he couldn't stand the sight of another horse ahead of him.

This time Jeff was ready for the blazing speed. But it was too much lead to overcome. Snow Flake was still ten feet ahead when they reached the school steps. Again Jeff had trouble stopping Goblin. When he trotted back Billy was already off Snow Flake and was telling the kids, "I told you that old nag was just a show off. I beat him easy."

"You should have," Hank said. "Goblin ran a lot farther and Jeff had trouble gettin' started. If Snow Flake had run that far he wouldn't of come in yet." Hank looked at Jeff, "Why'd you go so far past the turn? We could see you from here."

"I couldn't' stop Goblin. He wanted to keep right on running. I guess I'm not a very good rider yet."

Billy smiled a little. Jeff felt his cheeks burning. He knew Billy thought he'd deliberately lost the race because of the threat to beat him up.

Billy said, "I won. That's what the race was for. To see who could win."

"It was to see whose horse was fastest," Hank said. "And yours wasn't."

"I won," Billy insisted, "that's what I said I'd do. I proved you're still a clodhopper," he said to Jeff, "even with your fancy boots and big buckle."

One of the boys said, "Maybe you'll race Goblin at the Fourth picnic."

"What's that?" Jeff asked.

"The Fourth of July they have a big picnic in the field back of the church," Hank explained. "Everybody in the valley comes. There's all kinds of races and games and a baseball game and a horse race. Blackie's won the race three times. I'd sure like to see Goblin and him run."

"Yeah," the kids chorused, "Goblin and Blackie. Goblin and Blackie."

"Blackie'll beat him easier than Snow Flake did," Billy predicted. "If he runs you'll see."

"How about it?" Hank was excited. "You'll race Goblin at the picnic. Huh, Jeff?"

"I've never been in a regular race before," Jeff said.

"It's not much different than this was," Hank pointed out, "except there'll be maybe four or five more horses and they'll race a mile. First prize is fifty dollars," he added.

"I'll be ridin' Blackie, clodhopper," Billy said. "If you get in that race, I'll beat you worse than I did just now and in front of the whole valley."

"Go ahead," Hank urged. "You can beat 'im."

"I'll have to ask Dad," Jeff said.

"Crawlin' out of it," Billy sneered. "I knew you would. You're scared."

"He ain't either," Hank yelled. "Go on, show 'im, Jeff."

Jeff looked down into the expectant upturned faces and reckless anger boiled up in him. Not because Billy had called him scared. He wasn't. Because he'd challenged him in front of the whole school. Any excuse would look like he was afraid. "All right," he said. "I'll race on the Fourth."

"Good! You're in for another lickin', clodhopper." Billy swaggered off with Snow Flake toward the barn.

Hank walked beside Goblin that afternoon when they left school. As they passed the corner where the Decker pasture came down to the road the black colt raced to the fence. A pair of mares trotted out of the brush and joined them. They were the two Goblin had stolen from Lem Decker. They'd been with him the morning he was caught in the quicksand of Buttercup Canyon. Goblin nickered excitedly and headed for the fence. Jeff hauled back on the reins. For a minute they went round and round as Jeff pulled his head sideways.

"What's the matter with you?" Jeff said angrily. "You got in trouble stealing those mares before. You want Lem to come after you with a rifle? You keep away from them."

After they'd passed Hank observed, "When I get me a horse, think it'll be a mare." At the big rock he turned off and headed for home.

For the first time in two weeks Jeff went to the store. And for the first time ever he got there on Goblin. He stopped at the blacksmith shop. Al Alderman came out wiping his hands on the leather apron. He walked all around Goblin, looking him over. He found a loose shoe, got a hammer and nails, and replaced two nails.

Jeff asked, "You know anybody that might have a horse

like Goblin, Mr. Alderman?"

"Not in this upper valley, Jeff."

"What kind of horse is he?"

Alderman shook his head. "I'm not familiar with all the different breeds. My interest is mostly in a horse's feet. The ones I know best are cayuses and work horses, the kind we've got around here. But one thing I do know about this animal. He's quite a horse."

"I'm going to race him in the Fourth of July picnic. You think he can beat Blackie?"

"Only a race can tell that. But he'll give Blackie a run for his money."

"Yes, sir. How much do I owe you for fixing the shoe?"

Alderman waved a big hand, "One friend to another."

"Thank you," Jeff said and went on to the store. He was about to dismount and tie Goblin to the hitch rail beside another horse when Lem Decker came out with a handful of mail. He stopped and looked at the big horse, black brows pulled together in that perpetual scowl. Jeff sat still and looked back at him. The dread he'd always known in the presence of this big, somber man tightened his throat.

Fred came from the store and Lem said, "You figure to keep this animal?"

"Yes."

"Then you keep him up there. If this outlaw gets loose just once and bothers my mares again, I'll kill him on sight." He was looking at Fred, fists on hips, belligerent, challenging. Jeff saw his father straighten, his shoulders square. He could almost feel the sparks fly between these two as somber black eyes and sharp black ones clashed. Unconsciously Jeff compared the two men.

They were of equal height. Fred was as broad as Lem but pounds lighter. Lem was thick chested and waisted. His arms and legs were heavy. He looked rock solid. He reminded Jeff of a plow horse, big-muscled, slow, and tremendously strong. Fred was more slender, with a stringy toughness and quickness Lem Decker would never have.

84

Fred finally said, "Your privilege, Lem."

"Just so we understand each other."

"We do."

Without another word Lem got on his horse and rode off.

"Now you know where you stand with Lem Decker," Fred said.

"You think he'd really kill Goblin?"

"I'd bet my life on it. Lem's no bluffer." He patted Goblin's nose. "No trouble with him?"

"No." He didn't want to tell about the race he'd lost or the trouble when Goblin saw the mares. Anyway the business with the mares had been no real problem.

Lilian came to the door and asked in a worried voice, "Trouble with Lem? He looked belligerent."

"Just an understanding."

Jeff tied Goblin and followed his parents inside. "They want me to race Goblin against Blackie at the Fourth of July picnic."

"Who's they?" Lilian asked.

"Everybody at school."

"I'm not sure you can handle Goblin in a race," Lilian said. "You might be thrown."

"I've rode him at a gallop lots of times," Jeff said. Lilian looked at Fred, "What do you think?"

"Why not? That's several months away yet. Jeff's a pretty good rider now. With the practice he'll be getting he should be a lot better." Fred's eyes began to shine, "Goblin just might take Blackie."

"I'm not sure I like it," Lilian frowned. "We've had enough trouble with the Deckers without adding a — a sort of grudge race."

"It's about time somebody in the valley beat the Deckers at something. Maybe Jeff and Goblin are the ones to do it."

"It's not a race with you. It's a challenge because it's a Decker."

That's right. I say let Jeff race if he wants to. And he wants to."

"You — you men!" Lilian said angrily.

"That's us." Fred smiled at her and changed the subject. "Been thinking, why don't we try Goblin on that new buggy we've got out back in the shed?"

"I'd like that," Lilian said. "Do we have a buggy harness or whatever they call it?"

"Got a brand new one. Let's put it on Goblin now and take the buggy home tonight."

Lilian tended store and they took Goblin around back where Fred removed the saddle and started to put the new harness on. Goblin hunched and reared. He let fly with both hind feet and threw the harness off. Fred tried twice more with like results. Then he gave up. "One thing's sure, he's not broke to harness. Guess we'll have to get Harve to help us."

"When?" Jeff asked.

"He'll be down to the store in a day or so and I'll ask him."

That night Fred carried the harness home on his back.

Saturday morning Harve came to try to break Goblin to the harness. Goblin bucked it off again and again as he had with Fred. But Harve had infinite patience. He talked to Goblin in a soft, quiet voice, petted him, and tried again and again. "It's not that he hates it or anything," he explained to Jeff. "He doesn't understand what it is and he's naturally leary of it. So as he learns it won't hurt him he'll be all right."

There came a time when Goblin left the harness on while Harve led him around the corral. Then, because he was sure Goblin would not tolerate the buggy shafts, Harve fastened a long pole on either side of the harness. The moment Goblin felt them he went into a frenzy of kicking. But that passed and by late afternoon Goblin was dragging the poles around as if they'd always been there.

"That's it," Harve said, "let's go get the buggy." He took the poles off. They led Goblin to the store, hitched him to the buggy and returned home. "Acts like he's pulled a buggy all his life," Harve said. "This fellow's got brains. He reasons things out."

Next morning they went to church in their own buggy. They were dressed, Fred said, "fit to kill in their Sunday-go-to-meeting best." Fred sported his black derby and Lilian her white shawl and Jeff in his pressed and shiny suit. Fred and Jeff had washed the buggy so the red wheels and black leather glistened. Goblin was curried and brushed until his red coat was like satin. The buggy top was up because it was raining. Goblin trotted down the road as sedately as any churchgoing horse in the valley.

Things changed dramatically at school for Jeff. He still met Hank at the rock every morning. He rode and Hank walked. Hank didn't seem to mind as they poked along and talked. Goblin would prance a little and snort delicately and toss his head as if there was something he should be startled by. His sharp ears were constantly snapping back and forth as he looked about. The black colt met them at the corner of the Decker land morning and night. The two mares were usually with him. Goblin always acted up a little when he saw the mares, but Jeff got him past with little trouble.

Sometimes Billy Decker raced past them on Snow Flake, but now he ignored Jeff. Goblin's ears would jump forward. He wanted to take out after the disappearing Snow Flake, but Jeff always held him back.

Hank usually muttered darkly, "Just wait. Someday! Someday!"

Jeff was accepted. He was one of the kids. He played in every game and was even sought out. He ate lunch sitting in the middle of the group and sharing their talk. The few times Billy took digs at him Jeff ignored him. After lunch when he went to the barn to give Goblin his hay and to water him, some of the kids always tagged along. They fed him so many apples that Jeff had to stop them for fear Goblin might get colic or something. Goblin had brought about the whole change.

Spring buds along the willow branches burst into faint green leaf. Hank said Buttercup Canyon was a solid carpet of yellow. They finished lunch one noon and followed by Hank and Jean Wallace, Jeff ran down to water and feed Goblin. He burst into the barn and then just stood there refusing to believe his eyes.

Hank said, "Hey! Hey, where is he? What happened?"

Goblin's stall was empty.

The halter lay on the ground and the strap that buckled behind his ears to hold it on was still fastened. The rope was tied to the manger. Somehow he had backed out of it. Followed by the two others, Jeff raced through the dim interior of the barn calling, "Goblin! Goblin! Come here, boy." He was not in the barn. Jeff ran outside and looked about the pasture. There was Snow Flake and the half dozen other horses kids rode to school calmly feeding at the far end. But Goblin was not there. Goblin was gone!

- 8 -

FOR A MOMENT Jeff couldn't believe that Goblin was really gone. Jean said, "But how'd he get loose with the halter and all?"

Hank said, "He got out of the barn somehow and then jumped the fence. Kinda spooky."

Jeff remembered Lem Decker's threat and the mares in the Decker pasture which they passed morning and night. He ran back into the barn, grabbed the bridle off the wall, and rushed out.

Jeff raced past the front steps where some of the kids still ate lunch.

Someone yelled, "Hey, what's up?"

He heard Hank explaining, "Goblin's gone."

Jeff ran all the way to the spot where the Decker fence came down to the road. There his worst fears were confirmed. The two top rails of the fence lay some feet away splintered and broken. Off in the distance the black colt was feeding alone. There was no sign of the mares.

He found tracks where three horses had jumped the hole in the fence, crossed the road, and entered the brush. He followed the tracks and finally lost them on solid ground. But they were headed straight for Buttercup Canyon.

Jeff traveled as fast as possible, but it still took a long time. He stopped to rest twice before he reached the canyon. The floor was a yellow carpet of buttercups undulating gently to the stirring of a small breeze. The ancient, emigrant wagon trail showed faintly black against the yellow. Jeff had hoped he'd find them in the open as he had the first time. They were nowhere in sight. He headed for the far end of the canyon searching for hoof prints as he went. He finally found three fresh trails through the buttercups. Goblin was driving the mares straight toward the narrow end of the valley. Jeff waded the creek and hurried on.

Finally he entered the dark timber where the boggy land was and where Goblin had become entrapped. Fog tendrils drifted through the trees and there was the remembered stench of dead and rotting vegetation. He passed the spot where Goblin had been trapped. They had carefully circled it and gone on.

Jeff had the uncomfortable feeling that Goblin was bent on getting clear out of the valley this time. He had never been beyond this point and was tempted to turn back. The old fear he'd always had of the unknown dangers lurking here was very real again. But he had to find Goblin before Lem Decker did. Of course Billy would rush home to tell his father Goblin was loose and he'd pass the fence corner and see the rails had been kicked lose. Lem would waste no time coming after Goblin.

The walls of the pass continued to pinch in until, at intervals, Jeff could see them marching along on either side. He began to call, "Here, Goblin. Come on, boy. Where are you, Goblin?" His voice carried through the stillness and bounced in echoes against the walls. "Goblin. Goblin."

A deer leaped out of the near brush and sent his heart climbing into his throat. It disappeared in a couple of bounds. Rabbits scurried away through the grass. A pheasant ran ahead of him for a few feet, then sprang into the air cackling wildly. He surprised a half dozen ducks in a green, slime-covered pond. They rose into the air with a whirr of wings and fled down the pass.

He wouldn't have believed this pass was so long. He left the boggy land. The fog tendrils disappeared. The creek returned to being confined within its banks and ran clear and swift. The bad odors that had oozed from the earth were gone. But the timber and brush remained thick. He would have to be on top of the horses to see them. He didn't realize how long he'd been searching until he became aware the light was going out of the day. He stopped to rest a minute and think. Even if he turned back now he'd be caught in this spooky forest in the dark. He didn't want that. But Lem Decker with his rifle was behind him. He had to go on. He kept calling, "Goblin. Where are you, boy? Goblin. Goblin."

Dusk was settling in fast when the pass began to widen out. Jeff sensed that before long he'd be coming into the next big valley. Once there, Goblin and the mares could go any direction and he might never find them. He kept going knowing that when full dark set in he'd have to quit. Finally he stumbled into a small open glade and there they were.

He called, "Goblin. Come here. Come on, Goblin."

Goblin tossed up his head and nickered. The mares stood quietly looking at him. Jeff wished he had some carrots, or sugar cubes, or a bucket of oats to tempt Goblin. He moved slowly toward him, holding out his hand, talking in his quietest, most coaxing voice. "You've had me plenty worried. We're in a real mess now with you stealing these mares and Lem out hunting you. Why didn't you leave Decker's mares alone? I don't know how we're going to get out of this."

Goblin's ears worked back and forth as he listened. He tossed his head and pawed the ground. Several times Jeff thought he was going to bolt away. He stopped, but continued talking softly, and each time Goblin quieted down.

"Come on," Jeff said, "It's time to go home. We've got to get these mares back before Lem finds you." Finally he was close enough that Goblin stretched his neck and nibbled at his shirt. He permitted Jeff to slip the bridle on, then Jeff led him to a stump where he could mount.

It was no problem to round up the mares and start driving them home.

Dark caught them before they reached the familiar openness of Buttercup Canyon's wide floor. The walls and the giant trees made this a black, mysterious funnel through which he passed and drove the two mares.

The deep shadows made by trees, brush, and rocks were all strange and frightening. The silence was alive with small sounds he hadn't heard as he passed this way in daylight. There were tiny rustlings in the grass. Some large animal went thumping away. Brush quivered as at the passing of a slinky body. A bird cried sharply as it flitted ghostlike through the trees. An owl's "whoo-whoo" sounded eerie. He kept listening for the blood-chilling scream of a hunting cougar. But it didn't come. In the black silence he even heard the soft murmur of the creek running over its stones.

Through it all Goblin paced steadily along bobbing his head, sharp ears working back and forth as if he, too, listened and catalogued each sound. He snorted delicately several times. But there was no hesitancy, no fear in the big body beneath him. Jeff patted Goblin's neck and murmured, "I'm sure glad you're with me. I sure am." The ears came back to catch his soft words.

So Goblin and he drove the two mares before them and passed through the dark part of the forest and came at last to the canyon floor and the carpet of buttercups that shone faintly under the night's first stars and a rising moon. Jeff drew a deep breath and looked back. He could still see the dark shapes of trees, rocks, and their shadows. The stream ran like ink under the trees and disappeared. He knew what was in that forest now. It would never again seem so mysterious and forbidding, just quiet and dark and utterly calm. The same sights, sounds, smells, and animals were there at night as in daylight. It was a forest like all forests, full of wildlife and growing things. There was nothing to be afraid of.

He patted Goblin's neck again and said, "But for you I'd have lit out for home like a scared rabbit and never known it." Goblin's ears came back. He bobbed his head.

They forded the creek and started across the flat canyon floor. Almost immediately they met three riders. The riders stopped. Even at a distance Jeff recognized the bulk of Lem Decker. With him were Billy and Chad.

Jeff drove the mares up to them, trying to think of something to say or do to calm Lem's temper. There was nothing. He said, "I brought back your mares, Mr. Decker. I'm sorry."

Lem Decker sat there, a solid, black bulk in the saddle. He said nothing.

"He — he only broke the two top rails of the fence," Jeff stammered quickly. "I — I'll fix them tomorrow right after school."

Lem Decker leaned down, pulled the rifle from the scabbard under his leg, and levered a shell into the barrel. "Get off that horse, boy." His voice was deadly.

"It was an accident," Jeff said in a rush. "I don't know how Goblin got loose. It won't happen again. I promise."

"You're right. It won't. Get off the horse, boy, and stand aside. I don't want you gettin' hurt."

"No! No! I'll fix your fence." The words tumbled out. "I brought back your horses. You can't shoot him."

"Boy, I said get off."

"I won't." Jeff was ready to cry except he knew crying would do no good with Lem Decker. He leaned forward suddenly and put his arms around Goblin's neck. I won't," he repeated.

Chad had been edging his horse sideways. He had his rifle out. "I can get him right plum through the head from here, Pa."

"No!" Jeff hauled back on the reins frantically. Goblin reared and backed away.

"Pa, he's gonna try to run," Billy warned.

"I can get him easy." Chad brought up his rifle.

"Hold it!" Lem was leaning forward studying Jeff.

"Pa, we've got to do it," Chad insisted. "This stallion's gonna be no end of trouble. You know that."

"He won't," Jeff insisted. "He won't ever cause you any trouble again."

Chad kept moving his horse sideways, "Pa, let me..."

"Shut up." Lem didn't take his eyes off Jeff. "Boy," he grumbled angrily, "you're as stubborn as your dad. All right, get outa here and see that that animal don't get loose again. You understand me, boy?"

"Yes, sir," Jeff said. "And thank you. I'll fix your fence, Mr. Decker."

"Fix my own fence. Get on with you."

Jeff turned Goblin, dug in his heels, and galloped hurriedly away.

He was still a half mile from home when he saw the swinging eye of a lantern and came up to his father.

"Hank said Goblin got loose and you went looking for him."

"Yes." Jeff was still shaking from his encounter with Lem Decker. "He broke down Decker's fence and made off with the same two mares again. I found them and brought them back. I met Lem and Chad and Billy back in the canyon and they took the mares."

"Lem say anything?"

"He was going to shoot Goblin at first. Then — then he didn't."

"That was decent of him," Fred said grudgingly. "He had the right. You go on home, put Goblin in the stall, and give him a feed. We'll talk about this after supper."

After they'd eaten and milked they sat around the kitchen table while Jeff told them everything that had happened.

"Can't figure Lem not shooting Goblin when he feels the way he does about us."

"Maybe he's not as bad as you've thought," Lilian suggested.

"Don't fool yourself. Lem's tough, bullheaded and overbearing. He and his friends and relatives are committed to running us out of the valley any way they can. Killing Goblin would have been a good addition to what they've already done to discourage us." He scowled thoughtfully, "I wonder what stopped him."

"Whatever the reason we were lucky this time."

"We won't be that lucky again," Fred said, "Not with Lem."

"Maybe Jeff had better not ride Goblin to school any more."

Fred looked at Jeff, "Not unless he makes dead sure the halter's on tight and the barn door at school is closed and latched."

"The halter was on good," Jeff insisted, "and the barn door was closed and latched."

"There was something wrong," Fred reasoned. "A horse can back out of a halter. The door might have been closed, but it couldn't have been latched, or Goblin wouldn't have got out."

"I thought it was latched."

"When you found Goblin missing you were excited," Lilian said. "Maybe you took it for granted it was latched when it wasn't."

"I guess so. I'll make sure after this."

Later, lying in bed, Jeff went over the whole thing in his mind. He was sure the barn door had been latched.

Next morning when he rode past the Decker corner on the way to school new rails had already been placed on the fence. The two mares and the black colt stood, heads over the fence, and nickered at Goblin. Goblin tried to head that way but Jeff fought him past. "You almost got killed last night for stealing those mares," he said angrily. "Haven't you got any sense at all?"

Hank asked. "Where'd you find him?" And when Jeff told him, "You're sure lucky Lem didn't shoot 'im. Billy said he would."

Billy had just taken the saddle off Snow Flake and turned him into the pasture when Jeff led Goblin into the barn. Half the kids in school trailed Jeff and fired questions at him as he removed Goblin's saddle and bridle and put on the halter.

"Where'd you find him?"

"Did it take long to find him?"

"Did you have a lotta trouble catching him?"

"How'd he get loose, anyway?"

Jeff had been steeling himself for this ever since last night. Now he said loud enough for Billy to hear in the next stall, "He didn't get loose. He was turned loose."

"You didn't tell me that. How do you know he was turned loose?" Hank demanded.

"When I came out to water him at noon yesterday the door was closed and the latch was hooked. I had to unhook the latch to get inside. So he was let out and the latch was hooked again.

"I saw you unhook the latch," Jean Wallace said. "But who'd do a thing like that?"

"He would." Jeff pointed at Billy Decker. "He was the only one that left the room yesterday forenoon after recess. Goblin was there at recess. I looked in."

"You're crazy!" Billy yelled. "Your old crow bait backed outa his halter and got loose by his own self."

"I suppose he unlatched the door and let himself out and then latched it again. You let Goblin out. You were in a hurry and you latched the door again without thinking. You knew your dad said he'd kill Goblin if he got loose and caused any trouble. You hoped he would. You hate Goblin because he's ten times faster than Snow Flake."

Billy doubled his fists and dropped his head in his usual menacing stance, "You callin' me a liar?"

"Liar, liar."

It happened exactly as it always had before. Billy charged into him so fast he hadn't time to move and knocked him flat. Then he was on top pounding him with his fists. Jeff was squirming around trying to shield his face from the rain of blows and to wriggle from under the heavier boy when the bell rang.

"Come on," one of the boys finally yelled, "we've got to get out of here or Mr. Jacoby'll be coming to see what's wrong. You fellers can finish this fight at recess."

"You'll get it good this time," Billy warned.

Jeff got to his feet, brushed off the hay, and got his lunch pail and books. His nose was bleeding a little. He washed the blood off at the trough. Then Hank and he followed the rest up to the schoolhouse where Mr. Jacoby stood ringing the bell on the front steps.

Hank kept muttering under his breath, "That Billy. Someday! Someday!"

Mr. Jacoby glanced at Jeff then looked away. His lips were tight.

All morning the kids kept stealing glances at him and Billy

96

behind Mr. Jacoby's back. Through arithmetic and reading Jeff kept thinking about the fight. He'd done the very thing his father had cautioned him against. He'd stood there, flat-footed, like a dunce, and let Billy charge into him and bowl him over as he'd always done in the past. Apparently, all that bag punching and his father's instructions hadn't done any good. Maybe he was going to take another beating from Billy at recess. This time, he suspected, it would be worse than any of the others.

At recess every kid headed out behind the school. It was out of Mr. Jacoby's direct line of vision from any window and far enough away so he wouldn't hear. Billy wanted to fight in the barn but Jeff said no. Goblin was in there and the racket might scare him.

The kids made a circle, and Jeff and Billy faced each other in the center.

Billy began circling Jeff, fists knotted. "You're gonna be sorry you called me a liar, clodhopper."

Jeff said nothing. He watched Billy lower his head in the familiar gesture and suddenly charge. He waited. The last second he stepped quickly to one side and thrust out his foot. To his immense surprise Billy sprawled flat on his face. Billy jumped up, face red with humiliation and anger. He rushed blindly. Jeff repeated the performance and Billy went down again.

Billy got up slower and Jeff waited, watching him.

Billy lowered his head, shut his eyes and came at Jeff, windmilling his fists. Jeff backed away just as he had for weeks from the swinging sack. He stepped to one side, found an opening and hit Billy in the nose with all his strength. Billy's nose began to bleed. Jeff brought up a right between the flailing arms and hit him on the jaw. The kids began to yell. Jeff was keeping his head up, his eyes open. That was how he happened to see Mr. Jacoby. He was standing at the corner of the schoolhouse watching, smiling a little.

Billy rushed again and Jeff forgot about Mr. Jacoby. He moved around, reminding himself that he had to keep Billy from getting hold of him.

Billy managed to land a couple of wild, swinging punches. Jeff promptly paid him back by knocking him down.

Billy sat on the ground, panting, wiping blood from his nose.

Jeff asked, "You had enough? You want to quit?"

For answer Billy climbed up and rushed Jeff again. Jeff hit him in the eye and then in the stomach and he sat down hard.

"You want to quit?" Jeff repeated.

"No." Billy got up and charged again. He knew no other way to fight.

Jeff hit him but he couldn't stop him. Billy got his arms around Jeff and they fell to the ground. But the beating Billy had taken had tired him. Jeff rolled him over and climbed on top. He began to hammer Billy with both fists.

Billy hadn't the experience of being pounded and didn't know how to protect his face.

Every time Jeff hit him he yelled, "You want to quit? You want to quit?"

The kids were making such a racket he didn't hear the first, "Yes. Yes, I quit. I quit."

Jeff got off and Billy got slowly to his feet. His nose was still bleeding. One eye was beginning to puff. He panted angrily. "I couldn't hit you. Every time I punched, you wasn't there. If I could hit you, I could lick you." Then he turned and started for the school, stuffing in his shirt. The bell rang and the kids started running for the front of the school.

Jeff was tired and he was still shaking with excitement. But he'd never felt better. His mouth was a little sore where a punch had landed, but nothing else.

Hank walked beside him marveling, "I knew it. I always said, someday. Someday."

Hank's "someday" had finally come.

- 9 -

JEFF WAS ALWAYS one of the last to leave school at night because he was slow saddling Goblin. When Hank and he finally left Mr. Jacoby was standing on the porch. He asked, "Things seem to be going a little better, Jeff?"

"Yes, sir."

Mr. Jacoby nodded, "That's fine," and went inside. One side of Jeff's mouth was swollen so that his smile was crooked, but that was his only mark of the fight. Billy's eye had turned black and both his nose and mouth were swollen.

The moment Jeff walked in the store Fred looked at his mouth and asked, "Billy Decker?"

"Yes."

"Did you win?"

"Yes."

"For the love-of-mike, boy," Fred said annoyed, "give out with some information. What was the fight about? How'd you win? Tell us about it."

"I'd rather not hear," Lilian said. "You had a fight with a schoolmate. You beat him. And I don't like hearing about it."

"But, Mom, he turned Goblin loose so Lem would hunt him down and kill him."

"You're sure?" Lilian asked.

"Billy was the only one that left the room after recess, and Goblin was there at recess." He told them the whole story. "Jean Wallace remembered that I unlatched the door to get in," he ended.

"Why didn't you tell us this last night?" Fred asked.

"I wasn't real sure about unlatching the door."

"So you took care of Billy Decker yourself today," Fred said proudly.

"Yes."

"Your father asked you how you won," Lilian reminded him. "Tell him."

"I fought him just like I've been punching that bag. It worked." He described the fight punch by punch. Lilian moved a bolt of cloth, sat down, and listened.

"Good boy!" Fred clapped him on the back when he finished. "At least one of the family has struck a blow for fair play in this valley."

Turning Goblin loose was as low trick as I've ever heard of," Lilian said with surprising anger. "I'm glad you gave him a threshing."

"Look who's getting pugilistic," Fred laughed.

"Somebody has to fight for Goblin," Lilian insisted.

While things had turned for the better for Jeff, the same could not be said for his parents at the store. Fred and Lilian were still ignored by the same people. They came into the store for their mail, and traveled to Springfield to shop. It reached a point where Lilian and Fred were both on edge and began snapping at each other. Lilian boiled over one night at home after a particularly bad day. For the first time Jeff heard his father and mother on the verge of quarreling. Sharp words flew back and forth. Both were angry. He sat at the table still and miserable and a little frightened.

"Just how much longer do you think we can go on like this?" Lilian demanded. "Three out of every four people who came into the store today came for mail and nothing else. If it weren't for the post office we wouldn't be doing enough business to feed a mouse."

"It's not that bad," Fred said angrily. "You don't have to exaggerate."

"Exaggerate! Little by little every day the Deckers and their friends and relatives are freezing us out. Don't you see that?"

"I'm not blind. I know that what we get from the government for handling the mail and post office is all that keeps us going."

"That's just it. It's not keeping us going. It's just letting us go broke a little slower."

Fred dug fingers through his hair. "If there was just a bridge or ferry here to connect us with the people right across the river. They have to go seven or eight miles to Springfield to shop. If they could cross there we'd get their trade."

"Probably more of Decker's friends and relatives," Lilian said.

"Not according to Harve Sanders. The lost wagon train people settled on this side because they couldn't get across the river. Those on the other side came years later. They have no connection with this bunch, don't even know each other."

"Well, they can't get here," Lilian pointed out, so there's no use wishful thinking. The truth is everything's been against us from the day we came. I can't blame these people, really. I think I can even understand their not wanting an outsider. After what they must have gone through to reach this valley, living here together all these years, intermarrying. Our coming must be a little like having a stranger in the family. I have to admire their loyalty while I hate it."

"You mean bullheadedness."

"That, too. If there was any hope of breaking down those barriers, I'd say let's stay and keep trying. But there's no way, Fred. No way."

"What to you want me to do?"

"Admit we're licked," Lilian said quickly. "We've tried everything and it's done no good. Swallow your pride. Sell and get out while we can still salvage something."

Fred shook his head. His chin was set, stubborn. "Maybe pride's part of it. But I'm no quitter. I can't give up something I know can be good without putting up a fight. I can't pull up stakes and run just because the going's tough. If you're not willing to fight for a thing, you don't deserve it."

"How do you fight people who simply ignore you? You can't fight someone who isn't actively opposing you."

"You can. We are. We're fighting by keeping the store open, by refusing to quit or be driven out."

"Until we go flat broke?"

"We can hold out a while yet."

"Why?" Lilian demanded.

"Maybe something will happen and things will change. It did with Jeff. Goblin came and everything turned around for him."

"That's an awfully big maybe."

Fred spread his hands in a helpless gesture, "Lil, I have to try. I'm sorry."

Lilian's sudden smile was like the sun breaking through black clouds, "I know," she said gently. "I didn't mean to blow up. But the way we're being treated is so darned unfair." She rubbed a hand tiredly across her eyes, "We'd better find our own Goblin or the end of the rainbow or something in a hurry."

Fred put his arms around her and kissed her, "I know," he said. I know."

Days later Jeff rode down to the store after school one night and saw a man up the road squinting through a three-legged telescope-like thing, He rode up to look. The man was young. He wore high boots and had a roll of papers sticking out of a hip pocket.

He grinned at Jeff, "That's quite a horse you're riding. What's his name?"

"Goblin," Jeff said.

"Interesting name." The young man wiped the back glass of the telescope, adjusted it, and squinted through it again.

"Are you looking for something?" Jeff asked.

The young man smiled, "Yes, you might say that." He waved both arms in a scissorslike motion. Jeff looked the direction the telescope was pointing and saw a man across the river. He was holding some kind of pole.

"Are you looking for something special?"

"Yes, very special. Did you ever see one of these things

before, son?" And when Jeff shook his head, "It's called a transit, a sort of telescope on legs. You can see a long way with it. Would you like a look?"

Jeff got off Goblin and the man said, "Look through there. Get your eye up against the glass."

The man across the river jumped so close Jeff could see his mustache. The long pole he held had rulerlike numbers. "Gee!" he said. "It sure is clear. Thank you."

He watched a few minutes longer then returned to the store.

Fred and Lilian were sitting disconsolately side by side near the big stove in back. A small fire was throwing out faint heat. Jeff asked, "How is business?"

"Great," Fred grumbled, "You're the first person who's entered in over an hour."

"Forty-one people came in today," Lilian said. "They all came for mail. About nine or ten bought something. We sold a couple of sacks of flour, four pounds of coffee, a couple of yards of ribbon, needles, cloth to make a dress, nails, shells, a few other things. A really big day."

Jeff said nothing. Then he remembered, "Did you see the man up the road and the one across the river?'

"What's special about them?" Fred asked.

"The man on this side is looking through a telescope thing, a transit he call it, at a man across the river. The man on the other side has a long pole with a lot of numbers on it. They're looking for something special."

"Surveyors," Fred said. "Now what in the world... Maybe we'd better look."

The man was still in the same place looking through the transit.

Fred walked up the road to him. He talked to the young man several minutes. The man gestured and pointed. Then he took the rolled-up sheaf of papers from his pocket, spread them on the ground, and Fred and he bent over them.

Finally Fred shook hands and came back, walking fast. He bounced up the steps wearing a wide grin like Jeff hadn't seen in months. His black eyes fairly shot sparks.

"You can't guess what they're doing." His voice bubbled. "You wouldn't guess in a thousand years."

"Wanta bet?" Lilian's eyes were shining, too. Her voice had a lightness as if she were holding in something that wanted to explode. "Wanta bet?" she repeated.

"Sure," Fred laughed. "Name your stakes. Make 'em high."

Lilian folded her arms and smiled knowingly, "I'll bet the next thirty-five years right here. They're surveying for a bridge site!" Her voice broke with excitement. For an instant her features twisted up like she was going to cry. "They're going to build a bridge across the river right where that man's standing. Oh, Fred! Fred!"

Fred's face fell, "How long have you known?"

"Since you started walking back," she laughed. "It's obvious they're surveyors. He showed you a set of plans. His partner is across the river. He pointed to both sides of the river. I've seen surveyors work. It was obvious. When you started back you said 'bridge' with every bouncing, grinning step."

"Isn't it amazing?" he laughed. "Who'd have believed it. Like a bolt out of the blue. A bridge, Lil! A bridge! Ye Gods, a bridge!" He waved his arms grandly. He grabbed her and whirled her off her feet. "Yippee!" He shouted. "Yippee! That's our own special Goblin, our end of the rainbow."

"Stop it," Lilian laughed. "Put me down, Fred! You're acting like a clown and right out in public." She was trying to be severe but her blue eyes were dancing. "Be serious," she warned.

Fred put her down. He bent and kissed the end of her nose. "I'm serious," he laughed. "See how serious I am."

"Stop it," she said. "Who's building this bridge and why?"

"The county. They want to hook the road here with another about a half mile on the other side of the river. The bridge will be the link up."

"How soon will they start to build?"

"He says right away. It's to be a wooden bridge. They plan to have it finished by fall. You know what that means, hon?" Jeff could see the excitement building in his father again. "Once that bridge is in we'll get the trade from across the river. We're going to make it. We don't need the Deckers and their friends and relatives. All we've got to do is hang on until the bridge is finished. That's a cinch. Come on, let's lock up and go home. If I stay around here and watch those surveyors much longer I'm going to blow wide open."

News of the new bridge spread swiftly through the upper valley. It brought more excitement than the area had known in years. People came in buggies, wagons, horseback, and walked to watch the surveyors laying out their intricate pattern of stakes. Lem Decker came and watched, big fists stuffed into pockets, silent, scowling. Finally he entered the store, got his mail, and left without a word.

"He can't run us out now and he knows it," Fred crowed. "Lem's no longer king of the valley."

A few days later the Short Line left two railroad cars on a short siding near the depot for the bridge engineers and their crew to live in. Huge timbers and loads of planks and other lumber began to arrive and were hauled to the bridge site. The engineers hired all the local men they could find, and the bridge building was begun. Harve Sanders, Benny and Check Wallace, Gib Shelly, Johnny Walsh, Chad Decker and his three friends, and a number of other local men went to work. Jeff counted more than thirty men working there at one time.

The engineer's name was Charlie Harris. He was young and blond and slim. This was his first bridge. He took to stopping at the store almost every night to buy cigars. He talked endlessly to Fred about his one consuming passion, his bridge.

"Now this bridge," Jeff heard him explain one night, "will have a concrete pier on both sides of the river but none in the river."

"You're going to drive piling?" Fred asked.

"Can't. That bottom's bedrock."

"No piers, no piling. Then what?"

Harris laughed tolerantly, "Got the amateur stumped, eh? Well, sir, we're going to set bridge timbers right on that bedrock and brace 'em."

"All the way across the river?"

"All the way," Harris said triumphantly.

"That current's pretty swift," Fred pointed out."

"Took that into account naturally. Wait'll you see the bracing we use." He bit off the end of a cigar and lit it. "Why, man, you could hold up the world with the proper bracing."

"I suppose so."

"I know so. See you." Harris strolled out blowing clouds of smoke.

Fred watched him go up the road and stop to study the bridge site. Then he shook his head, dropped the twenty cents in the till, and said, "Let's go home."

All day sawing and hammering went on at the bridge site. The first pier was poured, the ramp built. Timbers were set on end in the river bottom and held with an intricate network of bracing. The bridge began to take form. Harris said to Fred, "Notice how solid those timbers are standing?"

Fred looked at the swift water boiling around the base of the timber and nodded, "You're right."

"Bracing, man. Good solid bracing," Harris smiled.

The spring rains slacked off. Hazel and maple burst into leaf. Everywhere Jeff looked men and horses were turning the rich black earth and planting spring grains. Goblin lost the long hair he'd acquired during his stay in the wild. Now, in this lower altitude, with the coming of spring, and with Jeff's constant brushing and currying, his red coat glistened.

Jeff liked to sit on the fence and watch the powerful muscles bunch and flow like water as he trotted or galloped across the pasture. He talked to Goblin by the hour and the horse would talk back to him in nickers and playful nips at his clothing. At such times the pride of ownership swelled in Jeff's heart until it was almost more than he could bear. Goblin ran and kicked up his heels these first spring days while Trixie watched and placidly chewed her cud.

Pheasants and quail were nesting in the thick grass and along the fence rows. On the way to school Jeff often saw tiny chicks ducking through the grass. Gray squirrels were thick. They scolded from fence tops and tree limbs. The two mares were no longer in Decker's pasture to tempt Goblin, but the black colt nickered a welcome morning and night.

On weekends, Jeff and Goblin explored the country. He had lost his fear of the dense forests and was confident no animals were there that Goblin could not outrun. Harve Sanders said Goblin had gained about a hundred and fifty pounds. At home Jeff left him out in the pasture all day with Trixie, but not at school.

The excitement over the new bridge died down. People noted the progress but no longer stood about to watch. The bridge brought a slight increase in business. Chad and his friends came in often after work. His friends bought. Chad looked around and scowled.

There were two weeks of school left when the school board decided the schoolhouse roof needed reshingling and the building painted. They planned a box social to raise the money. The event would be held at the schoolhouse.

Lilian spent most of that day fixing a box of sandwiches, cookies, cake and a whole fried chicken. Jeff watched as she packed the box, wrapped it in bright paper and tied it with a red ribbon.

"Why fix it up so fancy?" he asked.

"Do you know what a box social is?"

"Boxes of food."

"Well, in a way," she smiled. "All the women fix up nice looking boxes of food like this, or better. Then at the social they're auctioned off and the men bid on them. The box goes to the highest bidder. Then the man who bought the box eats with the lady who fixed it. The money they get for selling the boxes goes to buy shingles and paint."

"How does a man know what box to bid on?"

"He bids on any box he happens to like. He doesn't know who packed it or what's inside. That's part of the fun."

"It is?"

"Of course."

That night Lilian wore her white shawl.

"Are you sure this is important enough to bring that out?" Fred asked.

"Our first box social and the bridge going in," Lilian smiled archly. "You bet it is."

It was dark when they reached the schoolhouse. The yard was thick with buggies, wagons, and saddled horses. The windows were ablaze with light and people were going in and out the open door. The sounds of music from a fiddle, an accordion, and a set of drums filled the night. The silhouettes of couples dancing passed before the windows.

They tied Goblin to a tree and went in. Fred left Lilian's box with a pile of others in a corner. Two men and a woman sat on a platform that held Mr. Jacoby's desk. They were the orchestra. The school desks had been pushed into a corner to clear the floor for dancing. Chairs and benches ranged around the walls. A dozen or so lamps lit the room.

The Hunters found a place on a bench along the wall and sat and watched.

It was the first dance Jeff had ever been to and he was fascinated watching couples whirl about the room. Some he recognized, many he didn't. A number of the bridge building crew were here. Engineer Charlie Harris was dancing with a girl Jeff had never seen. Al and Mrs. Alderman swung past. A trickle of sweat tracked down the big blacksmith's face as if he were standing over the hot forge hammering a horseshoe on the anvil. He was resplendent in a checkered vest with a heavy gold chain looped across his middle. Benny Wallace was doing fancy steps with a young woman in the middle of the floor. Harve Sanders danced gravely, talking to his partner. It was the first time Jeff had seen the trapper dressed up. He looked a little ill at ease in a vest and tie. Lem Decker danced as he walked, heavy-footed, plodding, scowling even now. He steered a determined course as if he expected someone to try to block his way.

A minute later the music crashed to a halt. Benny Wallace jumped on the platform, held up both arms and shouted, "Everybody out and join hands for a mixer. Come on, fellows," he called to some of the bridge building crew that stood bunched up together, "grab a gal and let's go."

Fred pulled Lilian to her feet, "Come on."

Practically every adult in the room found a partner and was on the floor. The three-piece band struck up *Turkey in the Straw*. Benny clapped his hands in time to the music and began to call:

> All join hands and circle left,
> Circle to the right.
> Everyone to the center and back.
> You did it so well — do it again.
> Swing the lady on your left,
> Swing your right-hand lady.
> Do sa your corners all,
> And do sa your own.
> Turn your left-hand lady with your left hand,
> Right to your partner and left and right grand.
> All promenade.

Hank ran along the wall and joined Jeff. They watched the mass of couples whirl and promenade and skip back and forth in time to blasting music and Benny's shouted instructions. The room rang with laughing and shouting. The women squealed. The men stomped their feet and whistled. The lamp flames jumped. The chimneys trembled.

Hank punched Jeff and said, "Let's go outside. This ain't no fun."

Outside the boys strolled toward where Goblin was tied. Against the side of a wagon two men took turns drinking from a bottle. A little further on they passed another group. Jeff recognized Chad's voice. He made out the short figure of Billy.

"That dancing sure looks like hard work to me," Hank observed. "Don't think I'd cotton to it much."

"Me either," Jeff said. They stopped beside Goblin and stood petting him. Goblin nibbled at Jeff's shirt and blew his breath in the boy's face. Sound poured from the schoolhouse livening the night.

"Ain't decided what kinda horse I'll get yet," Hank said.

"You talked to your pa about it?"

"Not yet, but I will. I'm waitin' for just the right time."

"How'll you know?"

"I'll know."

The music changed. Through the windows they could see people forming into four-couple squares. Then came lively music and Benny's tenor voice:

> Alemande left and a right to your girl.
> Form a wagon wheel and make it whirl.
> The hub flows out and the rim flies in,
> It's a right and left and you're going' agin'.

> Now a right-hand whirl and another wheel,
> The faster you go the better you feel.
> Now the gents step out and the ladies sweep in.
> It's a right and left and you're going' agin'.

> Find your partner, find your maid,
> There she is! Boys — promenade.

Chad and his friends drifted toward them. They were almost to the buggy when they discovered Jeff and Hank and turned away.

At intervals there was a short intermission and men wandered outside to smoke and talk. When the music resumed they'd go back. Finally the music stopped for a long period, but no men came out. Hank said, "We'd better get in there. They're about to raffle off the boxes."

People filled the benches along the walls. The musicians had quit the platform and Benny Wallace was up there. The food boxes were brought in. The school desks were scattered around the room to serve, Jeff later discovered, as tables to eat on.

Benny yelled, "Ladies and gentlemen. I'll call you that, even if maybe some of you ain't. You all know what this social is for. We need a new roof on the schoolhouse and a new paint job. Now them shingles and that paint costs money. These here beautiful boxes gotta sell for enough hard cash to pay for it. So loosen up them purse strings, fellows, and let's have some lively biddin'. The first man here that bids less'n a quarter gets thrown out personally by — " he glanced around the room, "Al Alderman." He picked up the first box and held it aloft. "All right, you big spenders, gimme a bid."

The men crowded forward leaving wives and sweethearts sitting along the walls. The young, single fellows bunched together, pointed excitedly and talked among themselves trying to discover which boxes belonged to which girls.

A voice called, "Thirty-five cents for that box."

"Thirty-five!" Benny was aghast. "I've a mind to sic Alderman on you. Why, man, the box and wrappin' alone are worth more'n that." He hefted the box. "And by the weight there's plenty of good stuff inside."

"You sure it ain't rocks?" a good-natured voice asked.

Benny put his nose close to the lid and rolled his eyes toward the ceiling. "That ain't what this old bugle of mine tells me, and it never fails. Come on, you sports, you can do better'n that."

The bidding went to sixty, seventy, eighty. It sold for eighty-five cents. The winner, one of the bridge crew, paid the treasurer and took his box.

Gradually the pile of boxes around Benny dwindled. Fred bid on a couple but dropped out when the price went higher than he wanted to go. Finally Fred, Lem Decker, and two other men began spirited bidding on the same box. The two men dropped out leaving only Fred and Lem. Benny began playing one against the other to run up the bid.

To Lem he said, "I've got two fifty. You ain't lettin' a storekeeper snow you under?"

111

And to Fred, "I've got three dollars. You gonna let this sod buster freeze you out without a fight?"

Jeff saw color climb into his father's cheeks, the stubborn set to his jaw, and knew he was angry. Across the room Lem stood rock solid, stubborn, and determined. The box was no nicer looking than many others. Jeff knew it was simply that two men, who disliked each other, had met head on for the first time. Neither meant to back down.

The bidding went to five dollars. Quiet settled through the room. Everyone realized what was happening. It went to five fifty, to five seventy-five. Lem said six dollars. Jeff heard Lilian whisper without moving her lips, "Let it go, Fred! Let it go. Do you hear?"

Fred stood, fists jammed into his pockets. Benny baited him once, then sold it. Lem got the box for six dollars.

Fred finally bought a nice looking box for two fifty.

Lilian's box came up and there was an immediate bid of three dollars. No one challenged and Harve Sanders walked up and claimed it.

At last all the boxes were sold. The women hunted up the men who'd bought their boxes and throughout the room couples settled down to enjoying their contents.

Lilian looked around searching for Fred and said to Harve Sanders, "Good heavens, look!" Fred and Cora Decker were sitting down together.

Jeff ate with Harve and Lilian. Lilian said, "Harve, you knew that was my box."

"I saw Fred put it down," Harve grinned.

"You could have got it for less," she chided. "You just wanted me to feel good knowing it brought a good price."

"No such thing. I wanted to be sure I got it. I've eaten your cooking before."

They were still eating when Benny announced that they'd taken in eighty-nine dollars and fifty cents. "That's enough to shingle the roof, paint the building, and fix some of those rotten boards in the porch."

Lunch over, the desks were pushed back into the corner,

the musicians took the platform, and the music began again. "Everybody join hands and form a ring with the partner you ate with," Benny called.

Hank came over and sat down. "You wanta go outside again?"

Jeff shook his head. His stomach was full. It was pleasantly warm. The music and sight of the whirling couples were lulling him to sleep.

"Me neither." They slid down, backs against the wall, shoulders leaning together.

The last Jeff remembered was Benny's voice singing:

> First couple out to the couple on the right,
> Chase the rabbit, chase the squirrel.
> Chase that pretty girl around the world.
> Chase the possum, chase the coon,
> Chase that big boy round the moon. . . .

Then Fred was shaking him and saying, "All right, son. Let's go home."

The musicians were putting away their instruments. A couple of men were lining up the desks again. Several were blowing out lamps. People were getting into coats and hats and going out the door. It was strangely quiet. Outside, good nights were being called. Wagons, buggies, and horsemen were pulling out of the schoolyard and disappearing into the night.

Goblin nickered a welcome as they came up. He was glad to be heading home and trotted off at a brisk pace.

Fred asked, "Have a good time?"

"Except for when we got into those squares with the Deckers' friends and relatives. Then the air was pretty chilly. How did you happen to buy Cora Decker's box?"

"Saw her nudge Lem when it came up for sale. Figured it was hers. Wanted to talk to her. Never had a chance before."

"And you wanted to annoy Lem a little by eating with his wife. What got into you two on that bidding?"

"Some people don't like each other on sight. Lem and I

are like that and we both know it. Someday we'll have to settle it," Fred said thoughtfully.

Lilian said nothing for a minute. Then, "How did you like Cora Decker?"

"I think she's like a lot of others in this valley, against us, because Lem says so. But she was pleasant enough tonight. Lem's our problem."

It was a quiet spring night. The moon and stars were out. The only sound was the rhythmic clop-clop of Goblin's hooves. The road was flat and straight. Goblin knew the way. Fred let the lines hang loose and the horse set his own pace. Jeff nodded, half asleep between his parents.

The buggy dipped into a low spot. The traces slacked, then jerked taut as the road tilted up. The left-hand trace parted with a snap. The singletree whipped around hard and slapped Goblin a stinging blow on the leg. He leaped, startled. The singletree caught him again. The harness slipped sideways.

Fred yelled, "Whoa! Whoa, boy!" and hauled back on the reins. It was too late. Goblin was suddenly plunging through the night in terrified flight bent on shedding this crazy contraption behind that was hitting him unmercifully. Fred, standing now, hauled back on the lines with all his strength.

There was no stopping the big horse. His head was outstretched, mane and tail flying. He was in full stride.

For a hundred yards or so the buggy somehow stayed in the road's deep ruts. Then the wheels climbed the sides into the rough ground. It bounced and careened crazily. Jeff and Lilian clung to the sides. It hit something, teetered on two wheels, then righted again. It whipped left, then right, almost spilling them. The front wheels hit a rock. Jeff felt it going over and tried to jump. Then he was sailing through the air. The last he remembered were his mother's terrified scream, the pound of Goblin's hooves, and the slamming and banging of the overturned buggy.

- 10 -

LUCKILY JEFF fell into a patch of brush and the bending limbs acted as springs. He was groggy for a few seconds, then he wobbled up and began looking around. Off a little way Fred was bending over his mother. He ran to them. Fred was saying over and over, "Lil, you all right? You all right?"

"I — I think so," she said faintly. "My head hurts so. I don't think anything's broken. Help me sit up."

She sat up. Then she saw Jeff bending over on the other side and put out her hand, "Are you all right?"

"I'm all right. How about you and Dad?"

"Nothing wrong with me," Fred said. "A little shook up is all."

Lilian said, "I want to get up." She clung to Fred after gaining her feet. Then she steadied, "I'm all right now. What happened?"

"Trace broke, I guess. It scared Goblin and he took off." They looked down the dark road. There was no sign of horse or buggy.

Lilian said suddenly, "My shawl! Where's my shawl. I've lost my shawl!"

Jeff and Fred began hunting along the road. Jeff found what was left of it caught on a patch of brush. He untangled it and took it to his mother. Lilian held it and smoothed it a minute. Then she wiped her eyes and murmured, "Well, I guess that's it," and dropped it.

"You can make another, hon," Fred said. "The important

thing is nobody was hurt."

"Yes," she said. "Yes."

They were still standing there when the Aldermans pulled up. Fred explained what had happened and Alderman shook his head. "That don't make sense, not with a new harness. Lucky somebody wasn't killed. Climb in, we'll take you home."

Several hundred yards down the road they found the buggy upside down. Goblin was nowhere in sight. Alderman and Fred inspected the buggy. The blacksmith said, "One wheel's broken. Top's busted, too. I'd guess the front axle's bent. Can't tell much about the shafts until I can inspect 'em in daylight."

Lilian said, "Oh, our beautiful buggy. Our beautiful buggy."

"Goblin dragged it a ways," Alderman said. "Then he tore outa the shafts. Lucky it's not any worse. I'll come up tomorrow and get it. This buggy can be repaired so it'll be good as new."

Jeff asked fearfully, "What happened to Goblin? Where'd he go? You don't think he's hurt, do you?'

"There's no telling," Alderman said. "When a horse runs away anything can happen. I've seen them run head on into a tree and kill themselves. Then again we might find him standin' someplace waiting for somebody to come get him."

The men got back in the surrey and they went on, everyone searching the night for sight of Goblin. "No tellin' how far he mighta run bein' scared like he was," Alderman said. "But once he shook the buggy he should have lost his reason for runnin'."

When they turned in at the Hunters a few minutes later Goblin was standing at the end of the lane by the gate, waiting to be let into the barn.

Alderman said, "Let Jeff go get him. He knows the boy better'n anybody else. And take your time, Jeff. Talk to him, in case he's still scared and nervous."

Jeff walked down the lane and began talking to Goblin,

"You sure made a mess of our buggy," he said. "You didn't have to run. If you'd stopped when Dad said to, there wouldn't have been any trouble. Did you get hurt, Goblin. Did you, boy?"

Goblin nickered and tossed his head. He walked up to Jeff, nibbled at his shirt, and blew his breath in the boy's face. He was completely calm.

Jeff led Goblin into the box-stall. Fred lit the lantern and they looked him over. There wasn't a scratch on his sleek hide. Al Alderman removed the harness and inspected it. He held up the broken trace, "This didn't break. It was cut almost through with a knife or something sharp. The first yank broke it. Somebody didn't want you to get home in one piece. I'll patch it tomorrow. The rest of the harness seems to be all right."

Fred's face was set. His black eyes were snapping, "Somebody could have been killed. If I ever find out who did this I'll beat him within an inch of his life."

"You won't find out," Alderman said quietly. "And don't try. This valley's not like any place you've ever been before. You know how these people hang together. I know you've been having problems. I've seen it. Just be glad no one was hurt and let it go. Believe me, Fred, that's best."

Jeff was getting ready for bed later when he remembered something and said, "Dad, while Hank and I were outside Chad and his friends came by. When they saw us they turned and walked away."

"Was there anybody else out there?"

"Sure. Men were coming and going most of the time, standing around talking and smoking or wandering around."

"Then you can't prove a thing," Lilian said. "There was all evening for someone to do that. I'll bet half the men there were outside one time or another. Al Alderman is right. Forget it. I don't want to know who did it. They didn't accomplish what they wanted, if they meant to hurt us, or scare us out."

Fred scowled at the floor and said nothing.

Next morning, on the way to school, Jeff and Goblin

passed the upside-down buggy and its smashed wheel and broken top. That night when Hank and he returned, the buggy was gone. Jeff went to the blacksmith shop with Hank. The buggy was inside. Alderman had both front wheels off and was straightening the axle.

"Harness is patched and ready to go," he said. "Only thing wrong was that cut trace. I'm just about through with the axle. Ordered new shafts and a new wheel. I'll get 'em in a couple of days."

Jeff went on to the store. Fred was in back alone. Jeff asked, "Where's Mom?"

"She didn't come down. She feels pretty shook up."

His father's face still had that tight, angry look. Jeff wandered out and went up to the bridge construction. He sat on the bank and watched men swarming over the structure. The bridge was getting close to halfway across the river. Jeff sat there until Charlie Harris came from the engineer's shack and waved his arms as a signal that it was quitting time. Then he returned to the store.

Some of the bridge crew came in and bought tobacco, a few got groceries. One bought a shirt and pair of canvas gloves. Chad and his three friends came in. Chad leaned on the counter and looked around while his friends shopped. They all left together. It was getting time to lock up when Lem Decker came in for his mail.

Fred was behind the counter. Jeff saw the anger building in his father's black eyes as Lem clumped to the post office, opened his box, and extracted a paper and several letters. Fred waited until Lem was even with him then he said in a tight voice, "Lem, tell your friend who cut the trace on our buggy last night that if he meant to scare the Hunters out, it didn't work."

Lem stopped. The two men faced each other across the counter. Jeff felt his throat tighten. His hands became clammy. "Maybe you'd better explain that." Lem's voice was dangerously calm.

Fred leaned forward, knotted fists on the counter.

"Maybe that's not necessary, but I will. Somebody cut one of the traces almost in two while we were at the social last night. We had a runaway on the way home and wrecked the buggy."

"Anybody hurt?" Watching Lem's scowling face Jeff couldn't tell if he was surprised or not.

"My wife was battered up some. But she'll be all right. It's lucky nobody was killed. If I find out who did it, I'm going to nail his hide to the wall."

"So would I," Lem said. "But why tell me?"

"I figure you're as much to blame as the sneak that used the knife on that trace. Maybe more."

"How so?"

"It was one of your relatives or some friend of yours."

"You can prove that?"

"Don't have to," Fred snapped. "They've all been helping you try to freeze us out since the day we came. Now with the bridge going in they know it's not going to work. So somebody's getting dirty."

"What anybody else does don't concern me. I take care of me and mine and no more."

"You and yours means about half the people in the valley," Fred shot at him.

"Well, we've been here a long time."

"So long that anything the Deckers want is just about law with these people."

"Maybe they feel they owe the Deckers something."

"Those who came across the plains and were lost owed your father plenty. This generation owes the Deckers nothing."

"Maybe they don't see it that way. We don't cotton much to strangers comin' in and takin' over what we've built up. This's always been a mighty close-knit community."

"So close they even do your fighting for you," Fred shot at him.

Lem hunched his thick shoulders. His black head dropped exactly like Billy's did. His voice was menacing, "Hunter, I don't like you, never have. But I had nothin' to do

119

with that smashup last night. Nobody fights a Decker's battles. Whoever did that acted on his own. I'm gonna drive you outa this store and outa this valley one way or another. The bridge will make it a little tougher to do, but I'll do it. You can count on it. And when I do, you'll know it's me because I'll be standin' right in front of you every second." With that he stomped out of the store.

A few minutes later Fred locked up and they started home. Jeff rode Goblin, and Fred strode silently beside him. Finally he said, half to himself, "Lem had nothing to do with last night. I'd bet on it. Under different conditions there's a man I could like."

"Why?" Jeff asked surprised.

"Nothing wishy-washy about Lem. He stands straight, looks you in the eye, and tells you what he thinks of you. I like that."

"Oh," Jeff said. He was completely confused.

School was finally out. The last day they had a party with lemonade and cookies.

As Jeff started to leave on Goblin, Jean Wallace called, "Don't forget you're racing in the Fourth of July picnic."

"Yes, don't forget," Billy said. "This time I'll beat you worse than I did on Snow Flake."

"You will, like heck!" Hank yelled.

"I'll be there." Jeff clucked to Goblin and rode off.

With vacation here Jeff saw Hank only when he came to the blacksmith shop.

He saw Billy Decker once. But the boys didn't speak. Volunteers began shingling and painting the schoolhouse on weekends.

Day after day only small harmless cannon-puff clouds marred the infinite blue of the sky. Summer's full heat hit the valley. The young grain had reached such height that Jeff could follow the course of a wayward breeze skipping across a field.

Jeff and Goblin explored the valley for miles around. One of their favorite rides was up to Buttercup Canyon. That dark, mysterious forest had become a fascinating place, filled with all sorts of game and amazing things to see and experience.

They stopped once at the boggy spot where Goblin was trapped in the mud and Jeff said, "Remember this place? I sure do. But for this I'd never have got you, and Lem Decker would have killed you sure. We were both lucky that day." Goblin tilted one ear back to listen to the boy's voice.

They saw a bear once. It dashed through the trees and was soon lost to sight. They saw numerous deer. Each time Goblin pricked up his ears and trotted eagerly forward as if to make friends.

Goblin devised a game he played night after night. Often Trixie did not come to the barn to be milked. She'd lie at the far end of the pasture placidly chewing her cud, and no amount of calling and banging on a pail would bring her. Then Jeff would go to drive her in. That was Goblin's's signal to play. He galloped circles around them, mane and tail streaming. He tossed his head, kicked up his heels. He pranced. He charged at Trixie and Jeff as if to run over them. The last second he turned aside.

Trixie sometimes became infected by his antics. Such play was not good for a clumsy cow with a full udder. Jeff had to run at Goblin, waving his arms and yelling, "Go on, beat it! Leave Trixie alone."

Goblin would dash off pretending great fright, then whirl and charge back. He'd slide to a stop before Jeff and snort and toss his head. Jeff would hold out a sugar cube and say, "All right. Come get it." Goblin would lift it daintily and big teeth crunched down. Then he'd nibble at Jeff's shirt and nicker. After that he'd walk sedately to the barn beside him. Jeff was never sure whether Goblin played the game just to tease him and Trixie or to get his nightly sugar cube.

The bridge drew Jeff's endless interest. Almost every day he rode up, tied Goblin to a timber, and sat and watched men swarm over the structure, laying planks, stringing timbers, sawing and hammering, and bolting braces in place.

One day Harve Sanders led him out a narrow board

walkway to the end of the bridge almost halfway across the river. Jeff looked down at the boiling water thirty feet below while Harve pointed out where the bridge would land on the opposite bank and how the bracing held the upright timbers from being swept away by the racing current.

"How much longer will it take to finish?" Jeff asked.

At the rate we're going, the end of July will see us pretty close to done."

The word July brought Jeff up short. The Fourth was only a little more than a week away and he was supposed to enter the race.

When they got back to shore Charlie Harris stepped out of the shack and waved his arms that it was quitting time. Harve and Jeff walked as far as the store and Jeff told him about the race. "Billy beat me on Snow Flake because I couldn't get Goblin started quick enough. When I did I couldn't turn him fast to come back."

"You be home tomorrow night. I'll stop on the way from work. We'll see what we can do with Goblin."

The next night Harve stood an empty box at the far end of the pasture. "To turn him tight we need something for him to go around until he gets the idea. The first few times you may have to haul him around hard until he gets used to making a tight turn."

They started up by the barn and Harve used two flat pieces of board that he slapped together making a sharp gun-like crack. They'll start you with a pistol so we want Goblin to get used to taking off at a sharp sound, so he'll know what to do."

Harve stood close to Goblin and clapped the boards together. Jeff shook out the reins and yelled. The first time Goblin reared and jumped, startled. Then he got the idea. The instant the boards clapped he was off with such speed Jeff had to lean forward for fear of being blown off backward. He had trouble at the box. Goblin wanted to run straight on until he met the fence before turning. Jeff hauled him around and they tried it again and again.

By the end of the second evening Goblin was turning so short he knocked over the box.

They practiced every evening until the night of July third. Harve was well satisfied. "Takes to this racing like he'd done it all his life. He's ready for Blackie tomorrow."

"You think I can win?"

"Can't tell. Blackie's mighty fast and he can turn on a dime and give a nickel change. Billy'll be ridin' him. He knows how and he's light. Blackie's won every year he's run. He's the fastest horse this valley's ever seen. You wanta win pretty bad, huh?"

"I want to beat Billy Decker. I've got to beat Blackie to do that."

"You want that first prize money?"

"It's not that exactly. Everybody expects Goblin and Blackie to race. I don't want Goblin to look bad."

Harve ruffled Jeff's hair and patted Goblin. "Tomorrow afternoon we'll see."

The Fourth of July picnic was held in a grove of trees behind the church. The local baseball field was at the edge of the grove. There was a grandstand that would hold several hundred people. All through the grove lunch baskets were opened on blankets spread on the ground. It seemed to Jeff that the whole valley must be here. A reporter had come down from Springfield and was going about taking pictures and making notes. This day would be written up in the paper. It was always the biggest celebration in the upper valley.

There was a constant racket of ladyfinger firecrackers going off and an occasional dynamite-like boom of a giant cracker. Small youngsters dashed about firing cap pistols. The noise bothered Goblin. His sensitive ears jumped back and forth. His flanks quivered at any particularly blasting noise. Jeff spent a lot of time talking to him, petting him to keep him calmed. Off a ways, Blackie seemed calm. He was tied to the back of the Drury Surrey. He had been through this racket before.

The afternoon's festivities consisted of a pie-eating contest, foot races, three-legged races, potato-sack races, a tug-of-war, then a baseball game with a rival team from Pleasant Hill.

The horse race was saved for the last. Anyone could enter, but it was understood this race was for the young people. A boy could ride any horse, his own, a parent's, or a friend's.

By the time the baseball game was half over Jeff was getting nervous. The beginning of the eighth inning Harve and Fred went with him to saddle Goblin. Harve did the saddling. Across the way Lem was saddling Blackie with Billie and Chad looking on. Jeff studied the big black horse again. Now that the saddle was going on, Blackie was becoming interested. He showed signs of nervousness. His big head was up and constantly turning, sharp ears forward. If there was no other horse in the valley like Goblin, then certainly there was none like Blackie either.

Other horses were being saddled. Jeff was surprised to see Bob Lyons on a cream-colored mare. Bob waved and shouted, "Gonna be fun, huh?"

The baseball game ended. Jasper won seven to six. There was a flurry of shouting and more firecrackers went off.

Harve said, "All right. Now for the race. Let's go."

Fred boosted Jeff into the saddle, "Lots of luck, son." He patted Goblin's neck.

The two men walked at Goblin's head to the starting line which was situated at home plate. Lilian sat in the grandstand with the Aldermans. They all waved. Hank yelled, "Go get 'im, Goblin! Go get 'im!"

Six horses and riders lined up at the starting line. Harve said, "Now, Jeff, remember, get away fast. Don't fool around once that gun goes off, Blackie won't. Goblin can run. Let him make his own race. You just concentrate on staying up there and turning him fast to head back. This will be a mile, out to that maple tree you can just see in the distance, around it and back here. Blackie can make that mile in fast time. We don't know if Goblin can stick for that distance. It's all up to him."

Jeff was at one end of the line, Billy at the other. As they approached the starting line Jeff felt a tensing of the big body under him. Goblin's head came up, his ears shot forward. Jeff had the odd feeling that the big horse sensed what this was about. Jeff settled himself tighter in the saddle. He felt that Goblin was going to explode off the starting line with a speed such as he'd never ridden before. The horse was surprisingly nervous and anxious, a trait he'd not shown in racing Snow Flake.

Benny Wallace stood to one side, pistol in hand, waiting for the boys to get their horses up to the line and quiet. Advice was being called from the grandstand. Then it became quiet.

Jeff watched Benny. Benny held the revolver aloft, said, "Ready."

When it cracked, Goblin was off as if shot from a bow. Jeff swayed back in the saddle, caught himself, and bent forward. It seemed to Jeff that Goblin was in full stride in a couple of jumps. The ground streaked away beneath his flying hooves.

Jeff risked a glance at Billy. Blackie was a good two lengths behind but he was running powerfully. Goblin didn't dare let up. The other four riders were strung out behind Blackie. The big maple was coming forward with surprising speed.

Jeff reached the maple, rounded it close and started back. Blackie was a good fifty feet behind him. Now it depended on whether Goblin could run a fast last half mile. Jeff watched the earth flying away beneath the driving legs and held his breath, waiting for the first indication of tiring. But Goblin pounded on, powerful legs driving like pistons. There was no hint of hesitation, no slackening of his stride. The grandstand came swiftly toward them. Jeff glanced back. Billy was a good hundred feet behind and using the quirt unmercifully on the straining Blackie. Jeff heard the shouting of the crowd. Then he saw Harve and Fred. And there was Benny Wallace at the finish line. Jeff looked back as he crossed. Billy was still using the quirt on Blackie.

He pulled Goblin in. The big horse wanted to keep running.

Harve helped him off and held Goblin's reins. "Goblin would have run all the way to Springfield," he laughed. "Boy, you've got a horse here!"

Fred slapped Jeff on the back, "You did it, son. You did it." Lem yanked Billy off the heaving Blackie, tore the quirt from his hand and threw it away. "I oughta use it on you," he said savagely. "That's no way to treat a good horse."

"I had to, Pa," Billy wailed. "I had to."

"It didn't help. Blind man could see that. Blackie ran his best. It wasn't good enough. You was beat. That's all there is to it. You was beat good."

"I'm sorry, Pa." It was all Billy could do to keep from crying.

Jeff got the first prize. The newspaper photographer took his and Goblin's picture. "Will that picture be in the paper?" Jeff asked.

"You can bet it will. That was a mighty fine race your horse ran."

The crowd began to break up and prepare to go home. The celebration was over. They were hitching Goblin to the buggy when Lem came over.

He looked at Goblin, scowling. Then he said to Fred, "I'll give you three hundred dollars for that horse."

"He belongs to Jeff," Fred said. "It's up to him."

"How about it, boy?"

Jeff patted Goblin's nose and the big stallion nibbled his shirt, "He's not for sale, Mr. Decker."

"Three hundred is a lot of money. You could get another good horse and have a couple of hundred left over. No boy needs a horse like this."

"I'd miss him," Jeff said, "and he'd miss me."

Lem scowled. Then he muttered, "I guess so." He turned and walked off.

"Well," Fred said, "there's one thing the Deckers aren't top dog at, but it took Goblin to show them what it was."

- 11 -

FOR A FEW DAYS Jeff was in seventh heaven after having beaten Blackie. He rode Goblin to the store everyday and tied him to the hitch rail because he'd discovered that people who were not friends or relatives of the Deckers stopped to admire him. The picture of him with Goblin appeared on the front page of the Springfield paper. Fred pasted it to the store window. But after a day Lilian took it down.

"There's no sense rubbing it in," she insisted. "Things are bad enough here as it is."

"I'm tired sitting back and taking a beating from the Decker clan," Fred defended. "Jeff and Goblin are the only ones who've been able to lick them at anything. Sure, I want to crow a little."

"You're not taking a beating, not any more," Lilian said. "They are. That bridge a-building is giving it to them."

"Good old bridge," Fred smiled.

Day by day the bridge crept across the river. Now people came down to the bank on the far side to watch the progress.

"Customers," Fred pointed out, "waiting to get across. It won't be long now."

Jeff went up to the bridge everyday, sat on a lumber pile and watched workmen swarm over the structure. The deck was laid three quarters of the way across now. Several times after the crew had quit for the day Jeff walked out to the end and looked at the opposite bank that was coming so near. He put his hands on the upright timbers and stared into the boiling water. He could feel the pulse of the current like a heart beat.

Cora Decker stopped briefly one day and spoke to Lilian while Lem was getting the mail. Lem's back was turned and she said quietly so he'd not hear. "I'm sorry you lost that beautiful shawl in the runaway."

Lilian smiled and said just as quietly, "Thank you."

After they'd gone Lilian said angrily, "Cora Decker is a nice person. I could be friends with her if it weren't for Lem."

"Look who's going on the warpath now," Fred laughed.

As the bridge progressed, Jeff could see a kind of quiet excitement take hold of his parents. The tensions, the snapping at each other disappeared. Again there was laughter in the house. His mother's quiet cheerfulness returned.

Fred took to walking out on the bridge every night just before they went home. Jeff sometimes went with him. They stood at the tip end one night and the opposite shore was not more than thirty or forty feet away. "About two more sets of timbers," Fred said happily, "and an approach and she'll be finished."

Behind them Charlie Harris said, "Well, Fred, what do you think of it now?"

Fred looked along the bridge at the intricate lacework of bracing and scaffolding. "I couldn't understand how it would work without concrete piers. Now I do. You were right."

Charlie Harris blew a cloud of smoke and removed the cigar, "Like I told you, you could hold up the world with the proper bracing."

"I believe you."

"Of course," Harris conceded, "it's no Brooklyn Bridge. But it serves the purpose. The county had a certain amount of money to spend. This is what it bought. It won't carry anything but farm wagons and buggies, but it's not supposed to. Someday, when the county's richer and the traffic is heavier, they'll build a bigger and better one. But that day's a long way off."

"How much longer will it take to finish?"

"About ten days give or take a day or two. We'll start setting next to the last timbers in the morning."

"I'll be the first to walk across it."

"Soon as we get close enough, we'll throw a plank across to the bank and I'll come get you. We'll cross it together. Your first walk across my first bridge."

"I'm looking forward to it."

"So am I." Charlie Harris tossed his cigar into the river and grinned at Fred. The grin made him look young and eager and excited. "You've no idea how long I've been looking forward to it. I guess you've got pretty tired at times listening to me talk about this bridge." He ran nervous hands though his hair, "I've wanted to build bridges ever since I can remember. I've dreamed of walking across my first bridge a thousand times. Now, in a few days, I'll do it. It'll be the end of a long and very rough road, Fred."

"And the first of a good many bridges."

"I hope you're right."

Jeff rode up to watch them set timbers the next morning. He tied Goblin and sat on a pile of planking where he could see the crew working far out at the end of the bridge. They were preparing to set the next to the last pair of timbers on the bottom of the river. He recognized Harve, Benny, Chad, and Charlie Harris with a couple of his assistants.

Jeff saw Lilian come down to the store. She stood on the porch, shaded her eyes, looked toward the bridge, then went inside. The Short Line drew his attention when it came thundering and whistling through the valley on its way to Oakridge. A little later the first timber was set and they began bracing back to the bridge end to stiffen it. Another crew was working at getting the second timber in place.

Jeff saw Fred leave the back end of the store and go up the railroad track heading for the depot and the mail sack. A few minutes later he returned, the sack slung over his shoulder. At intervals a buggy or someone on horseback or afoot stopped and watched a minute, then went on to the store.

Fred and Lilian would have the mail sorted soon.

Sometime past the middle of the morning, Lem Decker and Billy came in the buggy. They stopped and Lem scowled at the crews working on the end of the bridge. Billy looked at Jeff but didn't say anything. Then they went on to the store and disappeared inside.

Jeff turned his attention to the bridge. They were adding bracing to the second upended timber. When they got that one firmly braced, he thought, Charlie Harris will throw a plank from there to shore. He would go get Fred and they would be the first two people to cross the bridge.

He was idly thinking what that would mean to all of them when a great shouting came across the water. Before his unbelieving eyes both upright timbers leaned, twisted, and fell gravely sideways into the river with a great splash. The whole end of the bridge began to sway. The swaying ran the length of the bridge like the undulations of a crawling snake. Jeff's first thought was that his eyes were playing him tricks. He'd been staring at the bridge too long. He shut his eyes tight for a second then opened them again. Men were shouting in terror. They were racing back along the bridge. They were falling, getting up, running again. Bracing snapped and cracked. It flew apart with rifle-sharp reports. Out near the end Harve Sanders was flung outward, arms and legs flailing. He fell end over end like a tossed doll and disappeared into the boiling water.

The bridge was falling!

The bridge was swaying drunkenly from end to end. An entire section of decking crashed into the river with a great splash. A half dozen running men went down with it. An outer section broke loose and fell sideways, dragging down section after section in a chain reaction like a string of dominoes falling. Men were being thrown into the river. Others were leaping.

For a moment Jeff sat rooted to the pile of timbers horrified. Then he leaped to his feet and began racing toward the store.

Jeff burst through the screen door screaming at the top of

his lungs, "Dad! Dad! The bridge is falling!"

Lem and Billy Decker were coming up the aisle from the post office. Fred and Lilian were behind the counter. For an instant these four people were motionless. Then they were running toward the door. Jeff remembered later that he'd been surprised at how fast big, stolid Lem Decker moved.

The second section out from shore was falling into the river as they gained the porch. The water was littered with broken planks, timbers, and bracing. Among all this Jeff saw the bobbing heads of swimming, struggling men. A couple of men scrambled up the riverbank in front of the store, soaking wet. A third was half carrying another. The injured man held his bleeding head with one hand and kept mumbling, "Oh, my God! Oh, my God!"

Fred said to Lem, "Get down to the river. We've got to go after some of those men or they'll drown. I'll get a line." He ran back into the store.

The next few minutes were like something out of a bad dream. Jeff and Billy followed Fred and Lem down the bank to the water's edge. Fifty feet out a man was floundering in the current. Fred waded waist deep into the river carrying the coil of rope. He yelled, "Grab it! Grab it!" and hurled the coil, holding on to one end. The rope sailed out, unwinding as it went. It splashed into the water near the man. He grabbed it. Lem waded out beside Fred, and they hauled the man in hand over hand. Lem caught him and half carried him ashore. His face was gashed. His legs were wobbly.

Lem pushed him at the boys, "Take him to the store. Hurry!" Lem waded back into the river. Fred had already tossed the rope to another struggling swimmer.

The man was groggy and would have fallen. Jeff got on one side of him, Billy on the other. They hauled and pulled him up the bank, across the road into the store.

Lilian had pulled blankets off the shelves. They wrapped one about the injured man and made him lie on the floor. "Will there be any more?" she asked.

"Plenty more," Billy said.

As the boys raced out again she began tearing up sheets to use for bandages.

Al Alderman was carrying a man up the bank. He laid him down and bent over him for a moment. Then he rose, shook his head, and went sliding down the bank to the river. Billy and Jeff looked in horror at the first dead man they'd ever seen. It was Charlie Harris, the engineer.

Men who'd managed to get off the bridge began arriving. They ran down the bank and joined Alderman, Fred, and Lem in rescuing men from the river. Some were carried, moaning and crying in pain. Several were unconscious, or dead, and were carried cradled in the locked arms of four men. All went across the road to the store.

Benny Wallace stumbled up the bank, blood running from a gash on his head. He started to wander aimlessly down the road. Billy and Jeff grabbed his arms and steered him across to the store. A half dozen injured men were already stretched out on the floor on blankets. Lilian grabbed a towel, pressed it to Benny's head, and said sharply, "Hold it there, Benny. Do you understand? Hold it."

Benny mumbled, "One minute the bridge left me. The next somethin' hit me an awful clout." But he was holding the towel as the boys ran out again.

Al Alderman waded out of the water carrying an unconscious man in his arms like a child. A hundred feet downriver two men had swum out into the swift current and rescued another who was clinging to a floating plank, shouting at the top of his voice, "My arm's broke. I can't make it. I can't make it."

Billy ran down the bank yelling to his father, "Pa, where's Chad? Where's Chad?"

Waist deep in the river Lem looked around, "Anybody seen Chad? Where's Chad? Anybody seen my boy? Chad? Chad?"

Fred pointed, "Out there!" A hundred feet out in the river a huge timber was shooting past. A black head bobbed low beside it. An arm hung limply over the timber. Fred shoved the coil of rope into Lem's hands and plunged into the current. It was the first time Jeff had ever seen his father swim. He was a strong swimmer. His head rolled. His long arms slashed the water with powerful strokes. The current swept the timber downstream. Fred chased it. Lem ran along the bank shouting encouragement. Fred was still feet short when Chad's arm slipped from the timber. He sank from sight. The next moment Fred's head disappeared. A few seconds later both heads bobbed up together. Fred had Chad and was fighting his way toward shore.

Al Alderman and Lem waded chest deep. Lem swung the coil of rope with all his strength. The end splashed into the water near the two heads. Then Fred had it, and Lem and Alderman hauled them in.

Chad was unconscious. They laid him on the riverbank and began working feverishly over him. He had apparently swallowed a lot of water. There was a broad gash on his forehead. One arm seemed to be broken.

After a couple of minutes Chad groaned, spit up water, and opened his eyes. Lem started to pick him up and he cried out in pain. "What is it, boy?" Lem asked. "Where's it hurt?"

Chad ran a hand over his chest and stomach, "Here," he murmured, "all over here, Pa. It hurts awful."

"We need something to make a stretcher so we won't shake him," Fred said. "He's probably got internal injuries."

Al Alderman stripped off his leather apron and they carefully worked it under Chad, making a sling. Then with Alderman behind carrying his legs and Fred and Lem on either side holding the edges of the apron, they carefully lifted Chad and carried him up the bank to the store.

Jeff noticed then that Billy was crying. "He's going to be all right," he said. "Don't worry."

"I know." Billy wiped his nose with his sleeve and began climbing the bank. "I — I thought he was d-dead at first."

A dozen men were stretched out on blankets on the store floor. There were gashed arms and legs, bloody heads and faces. Some had broken bones. Several, like Chad, lay softly moaning holding their arms across their chests and stomachs.

Two figures were completely covered.

Harve Sanders was sitting on an upended nail keg and Lilian was bandaging his bleeding head. She left off bandaging and went close to Fred and Lem. "We need a doctor," she said in a low voice. "We need one right now. Some of these people have internal injuries. I don't know what to do for them. We've got two dead now, and we could have more soon. And I could use some help, too."

Lem said to Billy, "Take the buggy and go get your mother. She's good at this kind of thing. Hurry it up."

Billy ran out the door and jumped in the buggy.

Fred headed for the telephone, "I'll call Springfield and get a doctor out here."

Frank cranked and cranked on the telephone. He listened, jiggled the box, and cranked again. Finally he slammed up the receiver, "Line's down again."

"Maybe we can find it," Lem suggested.

Fred shook his head, "That could take hours or all day." He looked at Jeff, "You got Goblin here?"

Jeff remembered Goblin for the first time since this nightmare had begun. "He's up at the bridge tied to a timber."

"Get him. You're riding into Springfield for a doctor."

"How'll I find one?"

"Get your horse and I'll tell you," Lem said. He bent over Chad, "It's going to be all right, son. We'll have a doctor here soon."

Jeff raced up the road, untied Goblin, and climbed into the saddle.

Lem was waiting on the store porch. He patted Goblin's neck and said, "Now then, listen close, just as you come into Springfield you'll cross the railroad track. Go one block past the track and turn left. Go two blocks on that street. Dr. Harry Richman's is the last house on the right in the block. It's a big, two-story white place. You'll see a sign hanging on a post in the front yard with his name on it. Can you remember that, boy?"

"Yes, sir," Jeff said.

"Good. He's a friend of mine. You tell him what's happened here. Tell him I said to drop everything and get out here as quick as the good Lord will let him." Lem put a big hand on his knee and Jeff noticed for the first time that he was not scowling. It was the way his eyes were set deep in his head and overhung by heavy black brows that gave him that appearance. "Boy," Lem said, "don't ride this horse to death. He's a fine animal and he'll cover those seven miles in good time. Set him to a gallop, then let him get his wind again. A couple minutes more won't matter a whole lot to these injured men. You got everything clear now?"

"Yes, sir," Jeff said.

"Good boy. Then get going." Lem slapped Goblin and the big horse leaped forward. Jeff was ready for the familiar rush of wind that blew him back in the saddle. Goblin seemed to sense the urgency of the ride. He set a blazing pace.

The road followed the riverbank for the first mile. This Goblin covered in a rush. Then it veered away and wound through a stand of timber. After another half mile or so Goblin slowed to a steady gallop. This was the first time Jeff had run him such a distance and he was surprised at the steady rhythmic pound of his long legs. Jeff wished they could stay in the timber all the way to Springfield. The coolness would help Goblin.

They ran out of the timber into an open stretch. The hot July sun beat on them. Jeff pulled Goblin down to an easy lope and held him there. A pair of cock pheasants sprang out of the grass and shot away. A band of quail, dusting themselves in the road, exploded in all directions. They passed an occasional farmhouse and open pastures where cattle grazed. A man in a field leaned on a shovel and watched him ride by.

They entered timber once more. Jeff immediately felt the coolness. He let Goblin go into a hard gallop. A deer bounded across the road ahead of them, its white tail bobbing. Jeff guessed they traveled almost a mile through the cool timber before they emerged into the hot sunlight.

Goblin was breathing hard. His neck was black with

sweat. On an upgrade Jeff pulled him down once more. He held him there until they broke over the top. Then he eased up, and Goblin picked up his pace. Ahead, the road rose and fell and turned and twisted. Goblin ate into it at a steady run. Jeff guessed they were well over halfway when he pulled Goblin down again.

"You're doing fine," he patted the sweaty neck. "Just fine." The sharp ears came back to listen. After a couple of minutes Jeff eased up on the reins.

They began to pass an occasional wagon or buggy. A man yelled after him angrily, "Hey, kid you tryin' to kill that horse?"

Finally houses began to appear. The road veered toward the unseen river, then back. At last he glimpsed the roofs of the town. They pounded across the railroad track, went straight ahead one block, then turned left. Jeff pulled Goblin in and began searching the houses as he passed. He spotted the sign in the yard while still half a block away: DR. HARRY RICH-MAN, PHYSICIAN AND SURGEON. He rode right across the lawn to the front porch and tied Goblin to the porch rail.

A middle-aged woman answered his knock and Jeff said, "I've got to see Dr. Richman right away."

She smiled, "All right, son." She glanced at Goblin, "My, you are in a hurry, aren't you? Come this way."

Dr. Richman was a small, neat man in a white jacket and wearing gold-rimmed glasses. He pulled the glasses down off his forehead and said, "Well, young man, what can I do for you?"

Jeff exploded. "The bridge fell down and there's a lot of people hurt. Two of them are dead. You've got to come right away."

"Whoa, back up," Dr. Richman said calmly. "Come where? What bridge? What are you talking about anyway? Take your time, calm down a little."

Jeff drew a deep breath and said more slowly, "I'm Jeff Hunter. My dad has the store at Jasper. The new bridge fell into the river this morning…"

"Hold it right there," Dr. Richman held up a hand. "I drove out there Sunday and saw that bridge. It looked strong enough to me. If this is some kind of joke, I don't appreciated it one bit."

The woman said, "Harry, the boy's horse is at the front porch. He looks like he's been ridden awfully hard."

"You rode in? Why didn't you telephone? I happen to know there's a line to that store."

"Dad tried to phone but the line's down again somewhere. It's down a lot. I had to ride. And the bridge did fall. We've got hurt people lying all over on the store floor. Two of them are dead. Lem Decker said to tell you to drop everything and get out there as — as fast as the good Lord would let you."

"Lem said that? It sounds like him. Then I'd better go." He pulled off his white coat and began stuffing instruments into a black bag. "Fill me in, boy."

While Dr. Richman rushed about gettting ready Jeff told him what had happened. "Take a little time to hitch up the buggy."

"Can't you get there faster than a buggy? They need you now."

"I don't have a saddle horse."

"The railroad gasoline speeder!" the woman said. "They were working down here a couple of blocks away when I went to the store."

"We'll go see." Dr. Richman headed for the front door. Jeff had to trot to keep up. On the porch the doctor looked at the sweat-blackened Goblin and asked, "Will that horse carry double for a few blocks?"

"I don't know. We can try." Jeff got into the saddle and swung Goblin sideways to the porch. Dr. Richman threw a leg over and eased up behind Jeff. Goblin's ears went back. His head started to go down. Jeff jerked his head up, slapped him smartly between the ears, and said sharply, "Cut that out. You behave." He kicked him in the ribs with his heels and Goblin obediently loped off down the street.

The speeder was still there. Four men were busily punching gravel under the crossties. Dr. Richman told a big, red-headed man about the bridge falling. He dropped his hammer, motioned to the speeder, and said, "Get aboard, Doc, and hang onto your hat. You're in for a ride." He said to Jeff," Better get your horse outa here. This thing makes an awful racket."

Jeff trotted Goblin away. The speeder motor started like a bunch of firecrackers going off. When Jeff looked back it was flying down the track. Dr. Richman was holding tight to his black bag with one hand, his hat with the other.

Jeff wanted to hurry going back but he didn't dare. Goblin had run a hard seven miles. He let the horse take his own time returning, with the result it was more than an hour before he pulled up in front of the store.

Dr. Richman had brought some order inside the store. Men still lay on blankets on the floor, but they were washed up and bandaged and for the most part quiet now. Lillian and Cora Decker were bandaging the arm of the last injured man. The two dead men had been wrapped in blankets and securely tied with rope. Dr. Richman was in a corner talking with Lem, Fred and Harve Sanders.

"We've got to get these people into the hospital," the doctor was saying. "When is the train due through here?"

"In about forty-five minutes," Fred said.

"Can you flag it down?"

"Of course."

"Then let's improvise stretchers and get these men out to the track."

They made stretchers of blankets and poles and carried six of the most seriously injured across the back field to the railroad track and laid them on the ground. Chad was among them.

Fred flagged down the train. They put the injured on the floor of the mail car. Jeff watched them load the two blanket-wrapped figures. One was Charlie Harris. Just last night he'd grinned and said, "I've wanted to build bridges ever since I can remember."

Lem came up to Jeff and said, "You and your Goblin did fine. Thanks." Then as if embarrassed, he turned quickly and got aboard the train with Dr. Richman, Cora, and Billy. He called to Harve, "Take my buggy home." The door slid shut. The Short Line pulled out.

The small group wandered back to the store and stood about. No one had anything to say. The excitement of the day had drained them of emotions.

Harve Sanders finally got into Decker's buggy and sat there looking up at the broken end of the bridge. "Charlie Harris' first and last bridge." Then he picked up the lines and drove off.

The others gradually disappeared leaving the Hunters alone. The store seemed strangely quiet. Lilian went about gathering up blankets, torn sheets, and bloody towels.

Fred said to Jeff, "You and Goblin did a fast ride. The doctor says you probably saved a couple of lives by getting him so fast."

"How is Goblin?" Lilian asked.

"He's fine."

"Good old Goblin," she murmured.

"We've got to get him home, wash him down, and give him a good currying and a big feed," Fred said. "He earned it this day."

A few minutes later they locked up the store. They stood on the porch and looked up where the bridge had been. Broken planks and bracing dangled from the section still standing. It was the only indication that a bridge had ever been building here.

Fred said thoughtfully. "Thirty feet from the opposite bank. That's all it lacked." He shook his head. "We came so close to making it, Lil. So close."

"Yes," she murmured. "So close."

- 12 -

JEFF SPENT an hour washing down, brushing, and currying Goblin. He said, "You did fine. No horse in the whole valley could have done what you did."

Goblin nickered softly and nibbled at his shirt. Jeff gave him two lumps of sugar and a big feed of oats and hay.

Lilian prepared supper and they ate in silence. They all felt let down and tired, but restless. After supper Lilian did the dishes. Fred milked Trixie and turned her out. Then they went into the living room. Fred got a magazine and sat idly turning the pages. Lilian got out some mending and sat under the light. She began to patch one of Jeff's torn shirts. Jeff puttered about the room. Finally he went out and checked on Goblin again. He was calmly eating hay.

When he returned Fred asked, "How's Goblin?"

"He's fine."

Fred laid the magazine aside and rose, "Think I'll turn in."

"I think we'd all better," Lilian said. "It's been quite a day."

Next morning when Jeff arrived at the store on Goblin, all the bridge crew that had not been injured were there. They were talking over what had happened to them personally during the bridge's fall and what had caused it to fall.

"There should of been concrete piers all the way across," a man said. "Whoever heard of buildin' a bridge that long without concrete piers."

"They should have started from each side and built toward the middle, too," another said.

"Maybe you're both right," Harve Sanders said. "One thing I do know, the water on that far side is deeper and the current stronger than Harris figured. We couldn't hold those last timbers. When they went, that triggered the whole shebang."

"It was some shebang," Benny Wallace said firmly.

"I tried to run back but the weaving caught up with me. Seemed like I kept running in the same place."

"Something cut my legs out from under me and then I was going down head first," Harve said.

One of Chad's friends offered, "I looked down between my feet and there went the edge of the bridge. I don't remember hittin' the water."

"I thought somebody was shootin' a rifle over my head. I looked up and here come a busted timber right at me."

"Maybe they'll build another."

"County can't afford it."

A dozen people gathered on the opposite bank and stood pointing across the river. "Be a long time before they get here now. If ever," Benny said.

Lem's hired man drove up to wait for the mail, and someone asked if he knew how Chad was. "Went in last night," he said. "Lem and Mrs. and Billy are stayin' in town so they can be close. He ain't good. Doc says internal injuries and maybe his back's bunged up bad. He might not walk again."

People came in buggies, wagons, or horseback. They walked to the broken end of the bridge, looked and talked and left. The parade of curious lasted most of the day.

The young newspaper photographer who'd taken the pictures and written the story of the Fourth of July celebration came. He took pictures and interviewed some of the men. He had Fred explain how he'd rescued men from the river, and Lilian how she'd laid them out on the store floor and patched them up. He asked Jeff about seeing the bridge fall.

"You're the boy who rode into Springfield for the doctor,

aren't you?"

"Yes."

"And you won that Fourth of July race, too. Rode the big red horse tied to the hitch rail. Thought I recognized him."

"Goblin," Jeff said.

"From what I hear that ride yesterday was greater than your win on the Fourth. You've got quite a horse there. How about a couple of pictures of you and Goblin?" He took half a dozen then got into his buggy and drove off.

The bridge crew finally drifted away. Most of the local people had been down to look. By evening when they locked up the store, the curious traffic had dwindled away.

Next morning when the Short Line dropped off the mail, the story of the bridge and Jeff's ride for the doctor was on the front page of the paper, with pictures of the broken end of the bridge and Jeff and Goblin.

Fred read the article several times. Finally he put the paper aside and said thoughtfully, "We're worse off than when we came here."

"How do you figure that?"

"We had a little backlog of cash when we came a year ago. Now it's gone. Lately I've been counting on the trade we'd get from across the river to pull us through."

Lilian put a bolt of cloth back on the shelf. "The Deckers seemed to have a change of heart yesterday. Lem was actually reasonable and cooperative. If the Deckers have changed toward us won't it make a big difference with a lot of these other people?"

"In time, possibly. But we can't count on it. Don't forget that yesterday Lem was scared out of his wits. He thought he was losing his son. He'd have cooperated with the devil himself. Today's another day. You were right a long time ago when you said, 'Why don't we admit we're licked and get out while we can still salvage something,' I should have listened to you.

"Well, it's a little late for salvaging much. I was the bullheaded one, hoping all the time that something would happen to change things. You faced facts. I didn't. I am now."

"Are you sure you're not jumping to conclusions?"

Fred shook his head. "I laid awake most of the night thinking about it. Lil, there's no pot of gold at the end of the rainbow in this valley for us. There's no sense waiting one day longer for the inevitable. I'm gong into town on the Short Line this afternoon and talk with a couple of realtors. Maybe we can sell and get out before winter."

Jeff asked, "Where will we go, Dad?"

"Back to the city where I can find a job of some kind."

"We'll take Goblin?"

"Of course."

"When will we go?"

"As soon as we can find a buyer. And the sooner the better."

Lilian turned abruptly and went to the back of the store. Her lips were trembling.

A kind of gloom settled over them. Several times Jeff could see Lilian was on the verge of saying something, but each time she pressed her lips firmly together and didn't. Noon came and passed. Lilian asked, "will you have to take any papers or deeds of sale with you?"

"Not today," Fred said. "Maybe next time." He glanced at the clock, "I'll have to go change clothes pretty soon."

A few minutes later the screen door opened and Lem and Cora Decker came in.

Jeff stayed where he was, in back by the post office. He watched as Fred and Lilian went to the front of the store to meet them. For a few seconds all of them seemed a little self-conscious. Then Fred asked. "Did you come in on the Short Line?"

Lem shook his head, "Borrowed a rig from a friend in town and drove out."

"How — how is Chad?" Lilian asked.

Cora Decker smiled, "He's going to be all right, but the doctor wants him to stay in the hospital a few more days. He's got a broken arm and some internal injuries. They'll heal all right with a little time and rest."

Lem said, "Doc was afraid at first he had some spinal injuries and might never walk again. But those pictures, those X-rays are sure great. Showed everything was all right. Nearly scared us to death though."

"I'm glad," Lilian said. "How are the others?"

"They're all going to make it," Cora said. "The only ones that died were those first two. Some of the others might have, if you hadn't bandaged them up and stopped the bleeding and things."

"You helped in that."

"Only a little. You did most of it. You had blankets spread on the floor, ripped up sheets for bandages and had half those injured men fixed up before I got here."

Jeff could feel the tension easing.

Lem said. "We want to pay for those blankets and sheets and things. You shouldn't foot that expense. And another thing," he said quickly, before Fred could interrupt, "we came down especially this morning to say something." Lem drew a deep breath. He was obviously embarrassed. "It was Chad cut the harness trace at the box social. It's been botherin' him ever since you had that wreck. He didn't figure for anybody to get hurt. Just wanted to help scare you out. He told me about it yesterday. Darned fool kid."

"It's over," Fred said. "Nobody was hurt."

"He's old enough to know better. Somebody could have been hurt bad or killed. A runaway's nothing to fool with. I've been in 'em."

"It's all your fault," Cora Decker told him with surprising spirit. "The boys follow whatever you do or say. You know that." She looked at Fred and Lilian, "I should have spoken up long ago. I'm sorry I didn't. But when I found out you had saved Chad's life, I — I just blew up and right in the hospital corridor."

Lem shook his head, "You sure did."

"Lem would have gone after Chad, if I hadn't," Fred explained. "I just happened to dive in first."

"I'd have gone all right," Lem agreed. "Then there'd of

144

been two drowned. You see, I never learned to swim. But Cora's right. She made me face some facts." Lem rubbed his chin and finally said, "This row between us never should have been. It was my fault, too. But Si Campbell is my cousin and it seemed like I should stick up for him against an outsider. You know how close-knit this upper valley is."

"I found out," Fred said.

"He had me convinced that the bank and you had worked together to get him foreclosed on. I should have known better. Si always was a convincing talker."

"And an out-and-out liar," Cora said sharply.

"That, too."

"What made you change your mind? I mean other than Cora tearing into you?" Fred smiled.

"Hanging around a hospital with nothing to do, a man has a lot of time to think. Nobody could have done more when that bridge fell than you folks. You pitched in and got people out of the river, tore up expensive blankets and sheets, and patched up those hurt men, including Chad, without a thought as to who they were. And that ride your boy and his Goblin horse made to get Doc was something. Those things don't tie in with the double-dealing stories Si told. So I went down to the Springfield bank that foreclosed on Si. I asked questions. I should have done that long ago. The banker laid it all out for me in black and white, figures, everything. Si was a fool, as well as a liar. He could have had a fine thing here with the bridge coming."

"What bridge?"

"Haven't you heard?" Cora Decker said. "State's doing it this time. It'll be built right, concrete piers."

"Are you sure?" Fred asked.

"'Course I'm sure. Got friends in Springfield that know all about these things. State wants this road and the one across the river hooked up. It'll be in tomorrow's paper. They plan to start soon, so they can get the piers poured before winter. Why, man, by next spring you'll be busier than a one-armed paper hanger."

Fred and Lilian looked at each other, amazed. Then they began to smile. It seemed to Jeff they got younger by the second.

"Who was it just recently said there was no rainbow with a pot of gold for us in this valley?" Lilian asked.

"Me," Fred laughed. "Who else? Me!" He grabbed Lilian and whirled her about. "We get the bridge? We've made it," he chanted. "We've made it. By golly. We've made it!"

"Stop it. Fred! Stop it. Put me down. People will think you're crazy."

"I am," Fred laughed. He set her on her feet. "I am, hon."

Lilian patted her hair, embarrassed, and murmured, "I never. Well, I never."

Cora Decker smiled, "I'd have done the same thing. Well, these are the things I'd like to have." She laid a grocery list on the the counter, "While Mr. Hunter is filling this will you help me pick out some yarn?" The same color as that beautiful shawl you lost in the runaway. If you'll show me the pattern I'll knit another to take its place."

Lilian's smile was the happy one Jeff had always seen before they moved here. "We'll make two. One for each of us." They disappeared into the yarn section.

Fred and Lem became busy filling the grocery order. Jeff went quietly up an aisle on the opposite side of the store, out the door, and got on Goblin. He rode up the road to the broken bridge approach and sat looking at it. He patted Goblin's neck and said, "We don't have to leave here now. Everything's going to be all right. You know what that means? You and I can ride all over this old valley. What do you think of that?" As it had with his parents a kind of tension let go inside him. He felt like whooping as his father had. "Let's you and I take a ride to celebrate." He patted the arched neck again. "I sure owe you a lot. So do some fellows in the hospital, too."

Goblin's ears came back, listening. He tossed his head and stepped out. The powerful legs were soft springs bouncing them along. Goblin twisted his head and snorted delicately as if he understood the boy's words.

They went far upriver following the curving course of the stream. The day was warm and still. Not a breath of air moved the leaves or the heavy grass heads. At intervals Jeff heard the soft buzzing of bees working industriously at flower heads, the drowsy talking of birds in the nearby brush. A gray squirrel ran out on a limb, flicked its tail, and chattered at him. Chipmunks scampered along rail fences. A kingfisher swayed on a limb over the river while he studied a pool's clear depth. A heron stood statue-still and watched them pass. Horses and cattle drowsed in sun-warmed pastures. In all the land there was not one discordant note.

The sun swung straight overhead and began the long drop toward the distant velvet-green mountains. Jeff squinted upward. His stomach told him lunchtime had passed. But he didn't care. Fred and Lilian would miss him but they wouldn't worry. They were too busy being happy about the new bridge.

He found a blackberry patch, pulled up and slid from the saddle and trailed the reins. "You can eat grass," he said to Goblin. A few berries were turning black. But most that he picked were still sour. He wandered through the patch eating what he could find.

Goblin moved about through the long grass carefully avoiding stepping on the trailing reins while he snipped off tender new grass shoots.

Jeff stepped into a soft spot, followed it, and came to a small, clear spring. He scooped out a depression, let it fill and drank. The water made his teeth ache. He led Goblin to the spring and the horse buried his nose in the water and drank his fill.

Afterward Jeff lay flat on his back on the sun-warmed earth, squinted up at the infinite blue sky marred only by lazy puff-ball clouds, and thought there couldn't have been a more perfect day for such good news to come to the Hunter family. He lay there a long time, pleasantly warm and drowsy, listening to the soft sounds of the earth and the steady snip-snip as Goblin ripped off the grass tops. Several times the big horse wandered over to him, sniffed at the boy, and drifted off again.

Finally Jeff roused. They'd soon begin wondering where he was. He got up, led Goblin to a downed log where he could mount, and started back.

Halfway there he came up with Billy Decker jogging along on Snow Flake. He pulled abreast and for several minutes the boys jogged along without speaking. Then Jeff asked, "Going any place special?"

Billy nodded, "Snow Flake threw a shoe. I've got to take him to Alderman."

There was silence again. Billy kept stealing glances at Goblin. Finally, "He sure is some horse. He'd of beat Snow Flake that time if you could have turned him."

"Snow Flake won," Jeff conceded. "That's what we raced for, to see who could win. Harve says half a race is how the rider handles his horse. I didn't do my half."

"You did on the Fourth, and when you went for the doctor. Pa says no horse in the valley could have done what he did. He just about flew."

"Sure felt like it to me," Jeff said.

They came to the store. Billy said, "Be seeing you."

Jeff watched him ride on to the blacksmith shop. He was glad their quarrels were over.

A strange buggy was tied to the hitch rail at the store. A gold blanket was rolled up on the seat. Jeff tied Goblin at the far end and went inside. A pair of city-dressed strangers were talking to Fred and Lilian. One was very small and trim. He had fiery-red hair. The other was older and stout. He had a drooping mustasche and wore a derby hat. A gold watch chain was looped across his ample middle. All four people looked serious. Lilian's eyes were very bright, as if she had been crying or was about to. She turned and went to the back and disappeared behind the post office partition.

Fred said, "Jeff, this is Jerry Mack and Mr. Charles Sullivan."

Jeff shook hands with both of them. Jerry Mack's hand was smaller than Jeff's but his grip was surprisingly strong.

The little man asked excitedly. "Is Fly-by out front?"

"Fly-by?"

"He means Goblin, son."

He's tied to the hitch rail."

Both men headed for the door. Jeff and Fred followed.

The little man, Jerry Mack, jumped off the porch and ran to Goblin. He threw his arms around Goblin's neck, put his cheek against the horse's face and crooned, "Fly-by! Fly-by! We'd almost given up on you. I'm so glad to see you. So glad!" He patted Goblin's neck and rubbed his ears and kept talking softly to him. Goblin nickered and nibbled at the little man's shirt just as he did with Jeff.

Jeff looked at his father. Fred turned his eyes away.

Mr. Sullivan joined Jerry Mack and ran his hands expertly along Goblin's neck and back and down his legs. He stood back and looked at him critically. Then he said matter-of-factly, "Gained some weight; about a hundred fifty maybe two hundred pounds. But he's in good shape. Good shape."

Jeff watched and listened, and a coldness settled in the pit of his stomach. For a minute he thought he was going to be sick. He felt the heat of the sun on his back. A warm breeze caressed his cheek. But the coldness kept spreading and spreading. He could feel himself beginning to shake inside.

Mr. Sullivan started to talk. Jeff didn't know if he was talking to him or his father, "Jerry and me couldn't give up. Not even after all these months when the chances of findin' him got slimmer and slimmer. He was too great a horse, too valuable. We advertised but we heard nothing. Finally we laid out a route from the spot where he got away that we figured he might follow. We've been checking it out ever since. We found where they'd tried to trap a wild stallion that had stolen a bunch of local mares. By the description we were sure it was him. It took a long time to get down into this valley because of all the false leads. But we finally made it. Then we saw his picture in the paper yesterday with that story of the fallen bridge. We knew our search was over. The story of his being lost was in all the big city papers. You didn't see it?"

"Ours is a small local paper, "Fred said. "There's practically no sports section."

Mr. Sullivan nodded.

"Not many people would have hunted so long," Fred said.

"Not many horses like Fly-by. Fact is, he may be the greatest."

Fred looked at Jeff then for the first time. "They've been looking for Goblin a long time, son," he said gently. "He's a very famous race horse. Mr. Mack, there, is his groom and exercise boy. Mr. Sullivan is his trainer. His name is Fly-by."

"Funny name for a horse," Jeff said.

"Guess you're right," Mr. Sullivan agreed. "Seems most race horses have funny names. But that's what he does — flies right by all the other horses."

"He sure flew by Blackie," Jeff said.

"I read about it. I guess you understand why we call him Fly-by."

"I like Goblin better."

"I imagine so," Mr. Sullivan said gently. "Your pa told us how you found him. The racing world owes you a big debt." He drew his hand from his pocket with a roll of bills. "There was a reward. It's little enough considering who the horse is. But it's all I'm authorized to pay." He held it out. "It's five hundred dollars, son."

Jeff kept looking at Goblin. He didn't reach out to take the money.

Mr. Sullivan handed the roll of bills to Fred. "There's enough to buy another good horse and have several hundred dollars left over."

"He was the best in the whole valley," Jeff said.

"He was the best in the whole United States last year," Mr. Sullivan said. "Jerry, why don't you put his robe on?"

The little man removed Jeff's old scarred saddle and bridle and put them on the porch. He went to the buggy and got a halter and the gold blanket. When he unrolled the blanket the words FLY-BY were appliqued on either side in blue silk.

Jeff looked at Goblin with the robe on. He didn't look

like his horse any more. He looked like pictures he'd seen of famous race horses.

Mr. Sullivan said to Fred, "We should be going. I want to make Springfield this evening in time to telegraph Mr. Mattox, the owner, and tell him Fly-by's been found." He turned to Jeff, "I'm mighty glad we found him; but I'm sorry, too. I know how you feel. Jerry and I love him like you do. Would you like us to go inside so you can say goodbye to him?"

"No."

Jeff went down the steps. The little red-headed man dropped the halter rope and stepped away from Goblin.

Fred went into the store and closed the door.

Jeff rubbed Goblin's ears and ran his hand down under the blanket and patted his arched neck. His throat was dry and thick. He swallowed hard. "You look like a race horse now, all right." Goblin bobbed his head. His sharp ears came forward listening. He nickered. He nibbled delicately at the boy's shirt with his big teeth. Jeff searched his pockets for a lump of sugar. He had none. "I always knew you were special, from the first time I saw you in the storm. We had some mighty good times. I won't ever forget." He patted the sleek neck again.

Jerry Mack took that for a signal. He picked up the halter rope and got into the back of the buggy. Mr. Sullivan climbed into the seat.

"You win a lot of races," Jeff said. "Maybe someday I'll come to see you." He patted the velvety nose, then stepped back.

Mr. Sullivan slapped the reins and said, "Giddap." The buggy moved down the road.

Al Alderman and Billy came from the blacksmith shop and watched the little procession pass. Billy started to walk toward Jeff. Alderman took his arm and said something. They went back into the shop.

Jeff watched the big red horse, the sun shining on the gold blanket with the blue letters FLY-BY , until he vanished at the turn in the road. Then he went into the store.

Fred and Lilian stood side by side behind the counter. Lilian said, "I'm sorry, honey. I'm so terribly sorry."

"Guess I always knew it'd happen someday," Jeff said. "He — he was too good to stay here."

"They'll take mighty good care of him," Fred said. "A great race horse like him."

"I know," Jeff said.

"I've got five hundred dollars here. It's all yours." Like the man said, you can get another good horse and have a lot left."

"Not sure I want another. It wouldn't be the same."

"Whatever you say, son."

"Anyway I had the best horse in the valley. We beat Blackie. Nobody else could."

"You had maybe the greatest horse in the world," Fred said. "You cared for him. Rode him for your own, even to school. No other boy in the whole United States can say that."

"I know." Jeff went to the back of the store and vanished around the wall of the post office. He sat on a stool and stared out the window at the bright, warm day. He could look beyond seeing into the blue of the sky. His hands were cold. He rubbed them together.

This wonderful afternoon had gone dead.

- 13 -

JEFF MOPED about unable to shake off his loss. He had trouble sleeping. He caught himself waking in the middle of the night thinking he heard Goblin nicker or kicking at the lower board of the gate. He sat in the open bedroom window for hours staring out at the dark land, the shape of the barn, the lane, remembering the first time he'd seen Goblin. He didn't go to the store. After Lilian left he wandered about the house, went to the barn, and fiddled about in the box-stall, or sat and remembered how it had been with his big red horse.

Everything had changed when Goblin came. The school year that began so badly had turned out fine. He hated to think of this fall without Goblin.

He father talked to him in the barn one night after milking Trixie. Jeff was leaning against the box-stall. Fred sat on the milk stool and said, "Son, that was a rough thing, having to give up your horse. But you're not the only boy who ever lost a pet."

"I keep thinking about him and missing him," Jeff said.

"Of course you do. That's natural." Fred broke a straw and stuck the end in his mouth. "When you gave up Goblin I was mighty proud of you. You handled yourself like a man. Now you've got to go on being a man. You've got to forget Goblin. I remember I once lost a dog. I felt about the way you do now. Then I got another dog and forgot him."

"I can't forget Goblin. I don't want to."

Fred tossed the straw away. "I guess I didn't mean forget

exactly. Try not to think of him being gone and how much you miss him. Remember the good things, the good times you had. You had a lot of them. Be happy for those. That's how life is, some good and some bad. It's never all one or the other. It balances out. If you think of only the bad it can kill you. So try to think of the good part and the bad gets less bad with the thinking. After a while it's just a dim sort of memory that doesn't hurt any more."

"I know," Jeff said. And he did. But it didn't help.

Lem Decker and Billy drove into the yard the next evening. The black colt with the star on his forehead was tied behind their buggy. They both got out and Lem said, "All right, Billy. This is your idea."

Billy said, "Hi." Then he seemed at a loss for words.

Jeff looked at the colt. He had pricked his hears forward watching. "You taking him someplace?"

Billy nodded, "Sort of." He scuffed a foot in the dirt. "I saw those men take Goblin the other day. I thought you might want another horse. You always liked Star."

"You'd like to sell him, Billy?" Fred asked.

Billy shook his head, "I figured to give him to Jeff. He's mine."

"That's mighty nice of you," Fred said. "But you can't just give him away."

"I don't need him, and Jeff don't have a horse now."

Lem took Fred's arm, "Come on in the house. This doesn't concern you and me."

"But Billy can't do that. He's a valuable colt. We can buy him."

Lem said, "The last couple of days I've learned to take a back seat once in a while. It's time you learned, too. Now come on in. Let the kids settle this themselves."

Fred looked at Jeff and Billy. He began to smile. "I guess you're right."

When they were alone Billy said, "You used to save your lunch apple and feed him almost every night. Remember?"

Jeff nodded looking at the pony. "I liked him fine till I got

Goblin."

"He won't ever be as big or fast as Goblin. No horse in the valley is. But he'll make a good little horse. Pa says he'll be faster'n Snow Flake."

"He can run plenty fast. I've seen him hightailing it lots of times."

"He's nice and gentle. And he likes you. That's why he used to come to the fence night and morning to meet you."

Jeff kept looking at the pony. He was sleek and curried. He coat shone. He had an intelligent face.

"He won't cost no more'n Goblin to keep and he won't never bust out fences. You won't have to worry about him stealin' other folks' mares."

"That was real bad."

"I know how much you liked Goblin," Billy went on. "But he's gone. You can't always be thinkin' about a horse you'll never see again, and that you didn't really own anyway."

"I guess not."

"Then how about us puttin' him in the barn?"

Jeff kept waiting for the exciting feeling of owning the black colt he'd coveted so long. It didn't come. This was a gift, a sacrifice for Billy. It could not be argued or dismissed. He nodded, "All right."

Billy untied the colt and they went down the lane, the colt walking sedately between them. "I call him Star," Billy explained, "because of that white star on his forehead. You can change his name."

"It's fine," Jeff said. "It suits him."

"He's not broke yet. But you can start any time now. He won't be hard to break. He's smart."

"I don't know anything about breaking a horse."

"I do. I helped Pa and Chad break Snow Flake. When you're ready I'll come help you."

"I'd like that."

They put Star in the box-stall, took off the halter, and gave him a feed of grain and some hay. Billy stood petting him, "You're gonna like it here, Star. You'll see. This stall belonged to Fly-by. What do you think of that?"

"You'll miss him," Jeff said.

"Not much." Billy closed the stall door. "I've got Snow Flake. I didn't ever plan to ride him much."

They walked up the lane together. Fred and Lem were standing outside. Lem and Billy got into the buggy. Billy said, "When you're ready to break him, holler."

"I will. And thanks. Thanks a lot. I'll take awful good care of him."

"Sure," Billy said.

"They drove down the lane and Fred said, "I wouldn't have believed it. Those Deckers are fine people. You just have to know them. So you've got a horse again. This time he's all yours."

Star was nice and friendly. Jeff let him out in the pasture next morning and within an hour he was on good terms with Trixie. Whenever Jeff showed up he trotted forward, expecting something to eat. Jeff put a sugar cube in his pocket. But when he was about to give it to him he didn't. He remembered how Goblin lifted the cube daintily from his palm. He fed Star, curried and brushed him, and cleaned the barn. But every time he looked at the pony he saw Goblin.

That went on for several days. He knew Fred and Lilian were watching him, but they said nothing.

Business began picking up at the store. The state sent out an engineer to look over the bridge site. He told Fred they planned to start soon.

Then one night it happened.

Fred went to the barn to milk after supper and Jeff trailed along. Trixie was not waiting to be let in as usual. She and Star were standing at the far end of the pasture. Fred called and banged on a bucket but she paid no attention. Jeff went to drive her in. For the first time since he'd come here Star was feeling frisky. While Jeff drove Trixie in Star galloped circles around them. He tossed his head. He arched his neck. He kicked up his heels throwing clods of dirt. He pranced and snorted. Trixie caught the fever and clumsily tried to imitate him. She stumbled and almost fell.

Jeff ran at Star waving his arms, "Beat it," he yelled. "Go on, get outa here and leave Trixie alone."

Star dashed away, head high, black mane and tail flowing, snorting and feigning fright. Then he came thundering back and slid to a stop a few feet form Jeff. He cocked his head. His sharp ears came forward.

Jeff smiled. Without thinking he dug the lump of sugar from his pocket and held it out. "All right," he said. "Come and get it."

Star advanced and lifted the sugar cube with the velvety touch of his nose. His big teeth crunched down. Jeff thought of Goblin and the countless times he'd done just this. A great longing went crying through him, then it was gone leaving only a distant, diminishing pain. He put out a hand, rubbed Star's ears, and patted his neck.

"I guess we'll have to start breaking you tomorrow," he said.

Star nickered softly and nibbled delicately at his shirt. Jeff put a hand on his neck. They walked to the barn together.

ABOUT THE AUTHOR

Walt Morey's life has been as adverturesome as those of his characters. He has worked as a boxer, construction worker, mill worker, shipbuilder, theater manager, and deep-sea diver. Born in Hoquiam, Washington, Walt has worked and lived in the Northwest settings for his novels. His love of nature and the wild, the land and the people, and especially the world of children and imagination stand out in his books.

Although he learned to read at a late age, he quickly turned to writing — first for the pulp magazines, for which he wrote short stories, and later for children, who became his primary audience.

Walt's books have twice won the Dutton Junior Animal Book Award, and his first book for young people, *Gentle Ben*, received an ALA Notable Book award before being made into a movie and television series. His *Kävik the Wolf Dog* also won the 1970 Dorothy Canfield Fisher Award. Walt continues to write and to be honored for his contribution to American literature.

Walt Morey and Peggy, his wife, live near Portland, Oregon, on the banks of the Willamette River, where they enjoy the wildlife of the waterway and the seasons of their orchard and the surrounding land.

COLOPHON

This book is a reissue, without changes, of the text originally published by E. P. Dutton & Co., Inc., of New York. In all other respects, this edition is original.

The cover design is by Judy Quinn of L.grafix in Portland, Oregon. The cover art is by Fredrika Spillman of Mulino, Oregon. And the overall design of the books in the Walt Morey Adventure Library was under the direction of Dennis and Linny Stovall of Blue Heron Publishing, Inc.

For this trade paperback edition the type has been completely reset in Palatino and Optima, digital typefaces by Adobe Systems Incorporated. The text was set electronically at 10/13 in Portland, Oregon by L.grafix on a Linotronic 300 Imagesetter and printed on acid free paper in the United States by Delta Lithograph Company.

An excerpt from another Walt Morey classic…

SCRUB DOG OF ALASKA

—

THE WHOLE mining community of Aurora named the pup. At first, when they were annoyed by something he'd done, they'd say, "That no-good scrub of Smiley Jackson's." But that was too long. They shortened it to "That Scrub!" which was the lowest form of no good. And Jackson agreed with them.

Jackson considered himself an expert. He was choosing pups to build a new team. He raised, trained, and ran dogs in the Alaska sled dog races. He studied each carefully, idly fingering the ugly scar on his cheek which pulled his lips upward into a gargoyle-like smile. He noted each pup's disposition, agility, alertness, and especially its courage. He'd already chosen the black pup Keno for his leader. But the wolf-gray scrub showed no promise that he would ever make a good sled dog. To Jackson he wasn't worth even a bullet. He took an ax to do the job and approached quietly from the rear.

Some instinct warned the pup. He glanced back — and leaped sideways. The swing threw Jackson off balance and he sprawled in the snow. The ax flew from his hands. The handle smacked the pup in the ribs, and he yelped in surprise and pain. Before Jackson could get up, the pup raced into the trees and disappeared.

Jackson could easily have followed the pup and disposed of him. But now the dog was gone he would no longer have to be fed. That was all that mattered. It was winter. In all probability the pup would starve or freeze to death, or fall prey to some hungry predator. In fact, he might be dead by morning. It was twenty below now, and the temperature would plunge lower as the night advanced.

But Jackson failed to take into account that there was wolf blood in this young dog's veins. The wild instinct for survival had been bred into him for generations. Now it came to the fore as the cold and hungry pup struggled off through the snow toward the cluster of houses a half-mile away.

Within an hour the pup found frozen table scraps in a garbage pile behind a house. They were hard to chew with his baby teeth, but he managed. At another house he watched from the protection of a bush as a man hung a sack containing meat on a nail on his back porch. When the man disappeared inside, the dog crept forward and looked longingly up at the sack. The sweet odor of fresh meat hung on the frigid air. Saliva ran in the pup's mouth. He licked his lips hungrily.

There was an empty box on the porch under the sack. He jumped onto the box and reared up against the wall, trying to reach the sack. His clawing at the wall brought an immediate rush of steps toward the door. He jumped from the box, fell clumsily, and rolled off the steps. He had barely scrambled into the inner gloom when the door opened. Feet tramped about in the snow. The man muttered to himself angrily, then went back inside.

The pup worked his way farther under the house and found warmth. The stove just over his head warmed the floor, which in turn brought warmth down to him. He spent a very comfortable night.

But for the lucky accident of diving under the porch, Scrub might have frozen to death.

The next morning he returned to Jackson's one-room cabin. Jackson was outside feeding the pups and saw him coming. He grabbed a stick and ran at him, shouting. Scrub fled back into the brush. By now ravenously hungry.

He returned to Aurora and visited the garbage pile. This time there was no food. He wandered among the other houses, found garbage piles with a few bites of food, and eked out a slim meal. The day was biting cold.

He went to the house where he'd spent the previous night. A man was outside cutting wood. When Scrub approached, he picked up a stick, hurled it at him, and shouted angrily, "Get outa here! Beat it!" The stick missed. Scrub ran away again. He had learned the most important lesson to his survival: man was to be avoided.

He slunk about searching for a warm place to hole up. He discovered another house he could get under. The hole was at the back where there were no doors or windows to give away his approach. By being careful, he could come and go with little fear of detection.

In succeeding days Scrub found an old shed with a pile of dried grass in a corner. Best of all, he later stumbled onto an abandoned mine test-hole. It was dark inside and the air smelled stale. But down in the earth he was completely protected from the weather — and man didn't come here. Food remained his biggest problem.

Stealth and cunning were part of his heritage. Pup though he was, clumsy and awkward, necessity forced him to become sly and clever. In time he learned to visit the garbage piles only at night. He learned that the back porches of houses were good places to watch. Housewives sometimes put hot dishes out to cool or to freeze and his delicate nose led him unerringly. Some porches had plain wooden boxes that served as refrigerators in which food was kept fresh. Sometimes a box was not tightly closed. More often than not he found it.

Soon Scrub was automatically blamed when food was missed or a food box was broken into. Often he was innocent. Other families had young dogs which ran free during their first months. They formed into a pack and stole whenever the opportunity arose. But since they were fed fairly regularly, they were seldom blamed. Scrub grew surprisingly on his lean, uncertain diet. But he was never the fat, roly-poly pup the others were.

Scrub's sides were thin, his thick gray coat matted. Young as he was, the wolf in him was becoming visible in his black-masked face. His nose lengthened. His jaws became wider, showing the promise of tremendous crushing strength. His eyes changed to amber and he had a wolf's trick of tilting his head down slightly and looking obliquely up at any object that caught his attention. His legs became longer, the bones heavy. His front feet seemed out of proportion to the rest of his body. He became particularly clever at dodging sticks or other missiles.

Someone might have shot him, but he still was Smiley Jackson's property. Such an act might have aroused Jackson's hair-trigger temper. He was a vindictive man and, in this small community, no one wanted to risk his wrath. So they tolerated Scrub and ran him off whenever he approached. The teeth of every dog and the hand of every man, woman, and child in Aurora was set against him — except one.

David Martin was a young, slender boy about fourteen. He had dark eyes and straight black hair. His smooth skin was neither light or dark, but something of an in-between olive. He went to the little one-room school with the rest of the Aurora kids. After school he hiked off alone through the settlement, carrying lunch bucket and books. He entered a trail in the snow that led through the trees.

The first time the boy came upon him, Scrub was trying to dig a rabbit from a burrow in the frozen earth. If he caught the rabbit it would be his first food in several days. He was industriously tearing at the hard earth when he heard the crunch of snow and jerked his head up. The boy stood a few feet off. Scrub started backing away, prepared to run. He knew what to expect. He was ready to dodge the moment the boy's arm would draw back to throw.

Instead, the boy spoke to him. "You look awful thin. I'll bet you're hungry." His voice was gentle and quiet. The dog stopped, ears pricked forward, listening. The boy advanced slowly, opening his lunch box. He held forth a sandwich, "Here, I couldn't eat all my lunch." Scrub knew it was food and saliva ran in his mouth. He licked his lips hungrily. But he could not let the boy come close. He kept backing away.

The pack of free-running dogs, led by the black Keno, came trotting through the snow. They spotted Scrub and started forward on a run. Keno was in the lead. The boy snatched up a stick and Scrub bolted away. He glanced over his shoulder as he ran, ready to dodge when the stick was thrown. The boy was turned, facing the advancing pack. He hurled the stick at them. It caught Keno in the side and brought a yelp of surprise and pain. The black dog turned tail and raced back toward Aurora with the pack at his heels.

Scrub stopped uncertainly. The boy came toward him again, holding out the sandwich. His voice was low and coaxing, "Come on. It's good. I'm not going to hurt you. Come on."

Scrub listened, looking obliquely up at the boy. He wanted the food desperately. But he could not let the boy advance beyond a certain distance. He began backing off again.

The boy stopped. "All right, I don't blame you for not trusting anybody. Here." He tossed the sandwich in the snow under the dog's nose. For a moment Scrub hesitated, but the aroma of fresh food was too much. He grabbed it and gulped it down, watching the boy carefully.

"You see, I don't want to hurt you," the boy said. "Why should I? I wish I had more to give you. Maybe I'll see you again. Good-bye." He disappeared among the trees.

Scrub didn't see the boy for several nights. When he did, the boy had part of a sandwich and a couple of cookies for him. Again he talked quietly, coaxingly as he held out the food and tried to approach. "You remember me. I gave you a sandwich and chased the other dogs away so you could eat in peace. Here's some more. Come on, come and get it." Once again Scrub could not let the boy advance too close. The boy finally gave up and tossed the sandwich and cookies into the snow. Again he walked away among the trees.

Scrub saw the boy often after that, and more than once the food he received kept him from going hungry. He began to make a point of appearing somewhere near the trail at the edge of the trees where the boy was sure to see him. There was always food for him, and the boy continued to talk quietly. Then one night the boy did not come.

Scrub hung about the spot near the trail day after day. He went into the trees where the boy always disappeared, but found nothing. Day after day he returned, sat in the snow beside the trail, and waited. He missed not only the food he'd come to expect, but the first faint feeling of friendship he'd ever known with a human. The dog in him craved this. A fresh fall of snow finally wiped out all sign of the trail. Then Scrub knew the boy was not coming and gave up waiting. He had to scrounge harder than ever for food now to fill the needs of his growing body.

Gradually the days began to lengthen. The sun swung higher across the blue bowl of the sky. Its brilliance carried the first faint warmth of spring. A chinook blew up from the south and began biting into the snow blanket. The first gray-green patches of tundra appeared. Crocuses pushed through the melting snow and spread their blooms to a softening sky.

Ptarmigans, rabbits, and weasels began to lose their white coats. A host of small animals came from burrows beneath the thinning snow and dashed about in a frantic search for food. They were happy to be out of their winter confines into the wide, big world again.

The river ice became scored and rotten. Water ran along either bank, beneath the ice and over its rough surface. Then one day, with a noise like thunder that brought all Aurora racing to the river bank to view the spectacle, the ice began moving inexorably toward the distant sea.

Birch buds burst along the edge of the woods and the first leaves shone pale green and satiny smooth. Great V's of geese, ducks, and swans began passing over. At times the sky was alive with their talking. A cow moose emerged from the brush followed by her spindly legged calf. They made their way slowly to the ice-free river.

Spring had come to the North.

Scrub entered spring half-starved and ragged. The change of season brought no improvement in his condition. This was not altogether due to the people of Aurora, who hated him and drove him from their houses and garbage piles. The pack of free-running dogs had made his life miserable by chasing him at every opportunity. They were worse with the coming of spring. They were bigger, more aggressive, and they were led by Keno. His special delight was harassing Scrub.

Jackson planned to make Keno the lead dog of his new team. He was all black and sleek from being well-fed. He was exceptionally strong and fast afoot, and he was a little older than Scrub. Keno and the others made a game of chasing Scrub and robbing him of any food he had found or managed to steal. Scrub hunted the nearby woods to add to his slim diet, but wild game was scarce this close to Aurora and the pack was always hunting, too.

Several times Scrub had lain in the fringe of brush near Jackson's cabin and watched, drooling, stomach aching as the musher fed his dogs. He had sneaked up to the cabin in the dead of night in the hope that some morsel had been missed. But Keno slept near the steps and sounded the alarm that brought Jackson cursing to the door with a gun. Twice he had shot at Scrub as the pup raced into the protection of the brush. Both times he missed. Most of Scrub's meager food came from prowling the yards and cabins of Aurora. When he found something, he'd slip into the woods, where he could hide and eat in peace.

Keno knew this and was constantly on the lookout for him. The moment he spotted Scrub with food the race was on, with the whole pack streaming out behind Keno and urged on by anyone who happened to see it. "Take him! Go get him, Keno! Get the no-good thief," they'd shout. Quite often Scrub didn't make the protection of the trees and had to drop his precious food in order to get away. Keno and the pack would stop and devour what he had worked so hard to steal. This happened again and again during the summer, with the result that Scrub added very little weight and muscle at a time he should have been storing it up to see him through the coming winter.

Then one day Scrub stole a haunch of venison from a back porch and was slipping off toward the trees. The pack rounded the corner of a house and Keno spotted him. Keno let out a bellow and gave chase. The pack followed, yapping and barking. Scrub dug out for the woods at full speed. Once there he could dodge about among the trees and try to lose them. But he was hampered by the size of the haunch and Keno gained steadily.

Scrub made the trees, but the black dog was so close that Scrub didn't dare slow up to dodge or twist. He fled straight away trying to outrun them.

Keno gained and soon was snapping at Scrub's flying heels. Scrub could have dropped the meat, raced on, and escaped, as he had done many times. But he hadn't eaten for several days and was ravenously hungry. This time, when he knew he'd be caught, he dropped his prize and whirled, head lowered, teeth bared to fight.

Keno piled straight into him and both dogs reared on hind legs, teeth slashing. For a few second the lighter, scrawny Scrub actually held his own with Keno. Then the heavier dog's weight and strength bore him down. Keno straddled Scrub, teeth fastened in his throat. That was the signal for the pack to pile on. They buried Scrub beneath their weight. Now Scrub was fighting for his life. Somehow he twisted from Keno's jaws and with a mighty surge came to his feet, snapping right and left. Then the pack rolled over him again. Teeth tore at his thin body. Keno was at his throat again when blackness closed over him.

A few minutes later the pack trotted out of the woods, tails waving as if nothing had happened. Keno carried the remains of the haunch, which was his right as leader.

The silence of death settled over the forest. In a small sunlit glade the torn-up earth and still, mangled form of a wolf-gray animal was the only evidence of the savage battle that had been fought here.

Scrub Dog of Alaska is an exciting tale of a boy, a dog, and survival against the odds in the wilds of Alaska. Along with other titles in the Walt Morey Adventure Library, it is available at your favorite bookstore or from the publisher.

The Walt Morey Adventure Library
from
Blue Heron Publishing, Inc.

The Walt Morey Adventure Library stands for the finest in juvenile and young adult fiction. Every title meets the most rigorous standards of storytelling excellence. Readers of all ages will enjoy these timeless, emotionally charged tales of action and adventure by the author of *Gentle Ben*, as well as new books by Walt Morey and others. The following books by Mr. Morey are the first offerings in the WMAL:

Gloomy Gus
Scrub Dog of Alaska
Runaway Stallion
Year of the Black Pony
Run Far, Run Fast
Home is the North
Deep Trouble
Angry Waters

These titles are available at your favorite bookstore or directly from the publisher for $5.95 each, plus $1.50 s/h for the first book and $.50 for each additional book (US funds only, by check, MO, or VISA/MC). Discounts are available for purchases of the entire Library or large quantities of individual titles. To order any of these books, or for a current catalog and price schedule, write to:

Walt Morey Adventure Library
Blue Heron Publishing, Inc.
Route 3 Box 376
Hillsboro, Oregon 97124
503/621-3911

BLUE HERON
Publishing,Inc.